'Mr Dexter,' Caroline said coolly. 'There is no point in my being here any longer.'

She continued, 'My professional services weren't needed in the first place, as far as I can see.'

'You're right. But I have other needs, Caro, and you are going to satisfy every last one of them.' Ben gave her a slow, thoughtful look. 'I suggest we stop pussy-footing around and start right now.'

'Now, why would I agree to that?' Caroline queried, her heart thumping wildly.

'Because you owe me for twelve wasted years.'

'Judging by your impressive achievements, the last twelve years can hardly be called a waste.'

'That's not what I'm talking about and you know it,' Ben said. 'I've had twelve years of wanting what most men want, a wife, a family. Of wanting a good long-term relationship and not being able to commit to any other woman because no one came close to what I remembered of you.'

Diana Hamilton is a true romantic and fell in love with her husband at first sight. They still live in the fairytale Tudor house where they raised their three children. Now the idyll is shared with eight rescued cats and a puppy. But, despite an often chaotic lifestyle, ever since she learned to read and write Diana has had her nose in a book—either reading or writing one—and plans to go on doing just that for a very long time to come.

Recent titles by the same author:

THE CHRISTMAS CHILD
CLAIMING HIS WIFE

THE BILLIONAIRE AFFAIR

BY

DIANA HAMILTON

First published in Great Britain 2001
Harlequin Mills & Boon Limited,
Eton House, 18-24 Paradise Road, Richmond, Surrey TW9 1SR

ISBN 0 263 82532 9

Set in Times Roman 10½ on 12¼ pt.
01-0901-43519

Printed and bound in Spain
by Litografia Rosés, S.A., Barcelona

CHAPTER ONE

'THE resemblance is quite remarkable, Caroline. You could have been the sitter—come here, take a look.' Edward Weinberg's slender, long-boned hands beckoned her and she put the guest list for the up-and-coming private viewing down on the beautiful, fastidiously uncluttered expanse of his desk and went to join him in front of the painting a uniformed porter had just brought up from the strongroom and placed on an easel.

Her employer's remark regarding the likeness was irrelevant, but she was consumed with curiosity to at last see the masterpiece that Michael, Edward's son, had acquired at a small, country-town auction a few months ago.

Carefully cleaned, painstakingly authenticated, the lost work by the pre-Raphaelite painter J. J. Lassoon had caused deep ripples of acquisitive excitement amongst the select band of collectors who could afford to pay serious money for the pleasure of owning a thing of covetable beauty.

Caroline had been in the north of England advising the new heir to one of the great houses on what he could dispose of, with the most profit and the least pain, to pay death duties, and had missed out on all the excitement.

'Which will be the more important, the prestige or the profit?' She glanced at Edward from black-fringed, deep violet eyes but his expression gave nothing away. He had the face of a mournful aesthete, his tall, elegant figure looked fragile enough to be bowled away by a puff of wind. But he was as tough as old boots. If she had been asked to put money on his true feelings she would have put prestige as his prime concern.

The London-based Weinberg Galleries had a fiercely guarded reputation for offering art and artifacts of the finest quality. The acquisition of the Lassoon painting could only add to his reputation.

'I'll leave you to ponder on that.' Edward smiled as he turned away and Caroline gave her attention to the newly discovered masterpiece only to have her breath freeze in her lungs because he was right. The resemblance was remarkable. More than remarkable. It was uncanny.

Set against a riot of lush greenery, the artist's model cupped a white lily in her curving hands and it was the very image of her, exactly as she had looked twelve years ago at the age of seventeen. The cloud of glossy black hair reaching almost to her waist, the youthful translucence of the milky skin, the thin patrician nose, the over-full rosy lips parted in a secret smile, the dreaming, drowning deep violet eyes. Dreaming of love, drowning in love.

Even the title was apt. *First Love.*

A shudder of bitter anger rippled down her spine. That was exactly how she had looked all those years ago when she had loved Ben Dexter with all her passionate being. So much love, she had thought she might die of it.

Yes, that was how she had looked before she had learned the truth, before he had turned his back on her and had walked away from their turbulent love affair, her father's money in his pocket, more money than the boy from the wrong side of the tracks had ever seen in his life, his gypsy-black eyes glinting with the satisfaction of a bargain well struck, his whip-thin, virile body swaggering with heartless triumph.

She swung abruptly from the painting. She felt sick. She wished she had never set eyes on the wretched thing. It had brought back memories she'd buried deep in her psyche, memories she would have to struggle to inter again with even greater determination before the internal, unvented anger could do more real and lasting damage.

Edward's immaculately barbered silver head was bent confidingly over the phone as she walked past him, avoiding her office, going to Michael's to discuss the final gallery arrangements for the imminent private viewing, only breaking off when her secretary, Lynne, located her on the internal line just before lunch-time.

'The letters are ready for your signature and the balance sheets from the accountants have just come through. Mr Edward will want to see them. Oh, and he wants you to stay on this evening. He left a message. He's got a client for *First Love*. The usual drill.'

Champagne and canapés, followed—if the client showed serious interest and was willing to pay top dollar—by an elegant dinner at one of London's more select eating houses. As Edward's executive assistant it was her job to ensure that the evening went smoothly, his to extol the virtues and provenance of the piece the client was interested in.

'So he's not putting it in the private viewing,' Caroline mused as she came off the phone. 'Someone must be keen.' She leant back in her chair and raised one finely drawn brow at Michael.

The private viewings were as near the vulgarity of a public auction as Edward Weinberg would allow. None of the items were ever priced but amounts were discreetly mentioned, offers just as discreetly made and just as quietly topped until, at the end of the day, the original sum mentioned would have rocketed sky high.

Though occasionally, a particular client would make it known that he was prepared to go to the limit, and above, to acquire a particular piece and a private evening meeting, as the one scheduled for tonight, would take place.

'The old man plays his cards close to his chest,' Michael pointed out. 'He must have put feelers out—or waited to see what came up after the heavier broadsheets published that photograph of the painting. Who knows?'

He lounged back in his chair, his warm hazel eyes

approving her elegant, softly styled suit, the gleam of her upswept black hair. Caroline Harvey was quite something. Beautiful, intelligent, articulate. And a challenge. Her beauty was cloaked in inviolability. He wondered if she had ever allowed any man past a chaste kiss at the end of a date. He doubted it. He picked up a pencil, rolling it between his fingers, and wondered what it would take.

She returned his warm approval, hers overlaid with affectionate amusement. Edward's son was stockily built, almost good-looking. He affected a casual style of dress—bordering on the sloppy. Mainly because, she guessed, he knew he could never compete with his father in the sartorial stakes so went the other way.

She gathered together the papers she needed and Michael said, 'Lunch? There's a new place opened round the corner, just off Berkeley Square. I thought we might suss it out.'

He was already on his feet but Caroline shook her head. Since his divorce, over twelve months ago now, they often lunched together when they were both back at base. To begin with they'd talked shop, but recently their conversation had reached a more personal level. Without actually saying as much, he had hinted that he would like their friendship to deepen into something far more intimate.

She sighed slightly. Approaching thirty, she had choices to make: whether to remain single, a career woman with no family, just a small circle of friends;

or whether to become part of a couple, have children, trust a man again…

'Sorry,' she declined softly. 'I'll have to work through. I'm going to have to squeeze in the arrangements for this evening and I'm already pushed for time.'

She worked quickly and efficiently, gaining enough time to leave an hour early. She needed to go home to her small apartment near Green Park, change and be back at the Weinberg Galleries in Mayfair by six-thirty at the very latest.

She would have rather spent the mild April evening at home with a good book, and that wasn't like her. She lived and breathed her work. But she wasn't looking forward to this evening and wasn't stupid enough to pretend she didn't know why. The sooner *First Love* was off their hands the better. The memories it had forced into the front of her mind tormented her. She had believed she had forgotten the pain of heartbreak and betrayal. But she hadn't.

She dressed carefully because it was part of her job to look as good as she could: claret-coloured silk trousers topped by a matching tuxedo-style top, a slightly lighter toned camisole underneath, garnet eardrops her only decoration, high heels to add to her five-ten height. And she was back at the gallery to approve the caterer's efforts before Edward and his client arrived.

'Elegant, as usual, Ivan.' Her heavily lidded eyes swept the small but exquisite buffet, concentrating on that because she couldn't bear to look at the painting on its display easel, cunningly lit by discreetly placed spotlights. Just thinking about it, the shattering resemblance that reminded her of the passionate but clueless young thing she'd been, made her feel ill with anger.

'There's no need for you to stay on.' She made herself smile at him. 'As soon as you've opened the champagne you can fade away. One of the security guards will let you out.'

She squared her shoulders, forcing painful memories to the back of her mind. It was only a painting, for pity's sake! Ben Dexter had meant nothing to her for twelve long years and the residue of anger she hadn't realised she still felt had to be nothing more than a self-indulgent fancy.

It had to stop!

'Everything's in hand for the private viewing later this week, I take it?'

'Saturday. Yes, of course.' Ivan gave the bottle of champagne a final twist in its bucket of ice and stepped back, his hands on his slim hips. He had a dancer's body and soulful brown eyes. Caroline wondered wryly how many hearts he'd broken in his young lifetime as the brown eyes flirted with her. 'Everything will be perfect, especially for you—for you, anything else would be unthinkable.'

'Such flattery,' she mocked. Everything would be perfect because he and his small, hard-working team were the best money could hire, and inside that handsome Slavic head lurked an astute business brain.

The small moment broke the unease of not wanting to be here at all, and she was grateful for that until, from the open doorway, Edward said, 'Caroline, my dear, let me introduce Ben Dexter. Ben, meet my invaluable right hand, Caroline Harvey.'

She closed her eyes. She couldn't help it. The panelled walls were closing in on her, the luxurious Aubusson tilting beneath her feet, the tumultuous beats of her heart suffocating her.

Ben Dexter. The man who had taken all she had had to give—her body, heart and soul—then, Judas-like, had sneaked away with her father's pay-off. She should, she thought savagely, be thankful that, unlike Maggie Pope from the village, he hadn't left her, literally, holding the baby.

She forced her eyes open, scrabbling for the slim hope that two men could bear that name, made herself look at him and met the bitterness in his darkly eloquent eyes, saw the slight, contemptuous curl of his handsome mouth, the proud lift of his dark head, and wanted to hit him for what he had been, for what he had done.

He'd been a thorn in the sides of the parents of daughters, the bad boy of the village, disappearing for months on end to goodness only knew where, reappearing with his wild, gypsy looks, his whippy grace, his devil's eyes, to quite literally charm the pants off the local girls!

Only she hadn't known that then, all those years ago. He'd said he loved her, wanted her for always, until the stars turned to ashes. And she'd believed him. Then.

She felt herself sway with the force of her anger, scathing words of condemnation bubbling in her throat, choking her. But Ivan's steadying hand on the small of her back brought her back to her senses, and she smiled for Edward, met Ben's cynical eyes as Ivan moved discreetly away, and extended a hand towards the man she despised, dreading the touch, the clasp of those slim, strong fingers on hers, the warmth of his skin.

'Mr Dexter.' The almost painful clasp of his hand pushed whatever inanity she might have followed up with right back in her throat. His skin was cool, yet it burned her. She couldn't pull her hand away quickly enough.

'Miss Harvey.' Formal. Yet beneath the veneer something about his voice, something sensuous, like dark chocolate covered in rough velvet, sent her nerve endings skittering to life. How well she remembered that voice, the things he had said...the wickedly seductive things...the lies, all lies...

He turned away, his mouth indented, as if he were mocking her, saying something to Edward now, casually accepting the flute of champagne Ivan handed him and strolling towards the painting on display. So he wasn't about to acknowledge the fact that they knew each other, that they'd made wild, tempestuous love during that long-ago summer when the world, for her, had been touched by magic.

Well, why would he? She hadn't explained that

they knew each other when Edward had introduced them because, heaven knew, she was deeply, abidingly ashamed of her younger, stupidly gullible self. And he'd probably forgotten her entirely. Just one in a long line of silly, disposable females who'd been only too eager to lie on their backs for him!

The deal had been done over the canapés and champagne. Caroline didn't know how the boy who'd been brought up by his widowed mother in a near-derelict cottage could have come by that amount of spare cash. Well, however he'd come by it, she figured the means would have been unsavoury. But she wasn't going to waste mental energy trying to work it out.

Edward was giving them supper in the exclusive restaurant currently in favour. Caroline faced Ben over the elegantly appointed table, watching him covertly beneath the dark sweep of her lashes.

Twelve years had changed him; his shoulders were broader beneath the expensive tailoring, his honed body more powerful, his ruggedly handsome face less expressive than it had been at nineteen years of age, his tough jaw darkly shadowed and his sensual mouth touched with a recognisable line of determination.

She shivered slightly and forced her attention to the sole in white-wine sauce she'd ordered. She hadn't wanted to come, had even, for a moment, thought of crying off, pleading the onset of a migraine as an excuse to cut and run.

But the moment had passed. She wouldn't let Dexter turn her into a coward.

Edward had ordered champagne. He never drank anything else. Hers, untouched, had gone flat. The relaxed conversation between the two men ranged over subjects as diverse as politics and the theatre. She was barely listening, just wishing the evening would end.

'And how did you become attached to the prestigious Weinberg Galleries, Miss Harvey. Or may I call you Caroline?'

The hateful drawl pricked her violently back into full awareness. The question could have been interpreted as an insult, implying amazement that any respected firm would employ her!

'Through the usual route, Mr Dexter.' Her eyes clashed with his. If there'd been a hidden slur behind his words then he'd better realise she was up to any challenge. 'A postgraduate course in the history of art, alongside another in museum studies.' She laid her cutlery down, not bothering to hide the fact that she'd barely touched her fish. 'Fortuitously, Edward was looking for an assistant. I happened to fill the bill.'

'A dedicated career woman? Never married, Caroline?'

She caught the dark glitter of his eyes. He had never called her Caroline, saying that he'd have needed a mouthful of plums before he could have pronounced it properly. He'd called her Caro. Softly, sweetly, oh, so seductively.

Her heart thudded painfully. Oh, to have the ability

to erase memories at will! She made her voice cool, disdainful, 'No, I've yet to meet the man who could satisfy my exacting standards. And you, Mr Dexter—are you married?'

She saw his mouth tighten. She'd touched a nerve. Just feet away, she felt rather than saw Edward frown. One was not supposed to descend to personal levels with clients!

Tough. Dexter had started it.

'The married state has never appealed. I'm not into voluntary entrapment.' Urbanely said. The prick of annoyance obviously forgotten, his slow smile was unsettling.

No, you prefer to change your women as often as you change your socks. The words were on the tip of her tongue but she swallowed them. Spit them out and she'd be fired on the spot.

Taking advantage of the waiter's arrival to clear their plates, she excused herself and headed for the rest room. Of course he recognised her, she'd seen it in his eyes. She hadn't changed much. She had fined down a little, had acquired a veneer of sophistication, had cut her hair to shoulder length and had coiled it into a smooth knot on top of her head.

So she must have had something memorable about her, she thought wryly. Or did he remember the faces of all the women he had bedded and had discarded over the years?

It wasn't important, she told herself as she held her wrists under the cold tap to cool down. A few more minutes of his miserable company and she would never see him again. Then she took her mobile from her slim leather bag and called the cab firm she always used.

Moments later, she slid back into her seat. Edward handed her the dessert menu but she closed it and laid it down on the table. 'I'll pass,' she told him. 'And leave you two to enjoy the rest of your meal. I've a hectic day tomorrow.' No problem there, Edward knew what her workload was like, especially when there was an invitation-only viewing on the horizon.

She got fluidly to her feet, putting on a polite, social smile. 'So nice to have met you, Mr Dexter.'

Both men had risen. Ben Dexter said smoothly, bland self-assurance in his dark, honeyed voice, 'Humour me, Miss Harvey. My driver's due to pick me up in ten minutes. I'll drop you off. We'll have coffee while we wait.'

Once she would have tied knots in herself for him. Now she took great satisfaction in telling him sweetly, 'How kind. But my usual minicab driver is probably already parked outside. Enjoy your coffee.'

And allowed herself a small smile of satisfaction before she swept out.

She had no idea why he'd offered to drive her home. She certainly couldn't accuse him of having gentlemanly instincts! And he could hardly have wanted to reminisce over old times. Whatever, she had very politely pushed his offer back down his throat.

It was high time Ben Dexter learned he couldn't always get what he wanted.

CHAPTER TWO

THE alarm clock was a welcome intrusion. Caroline rolled over, silenced it, and slid her feet out of bed. She'd had a lousy night.

Dreams or, more specifically, nightmares of Ben Dexter weren't conducive to restful sleep. Especially when they featured such graphic images as his sweat-slicked olive skin against the white femininity of hers, his mouth exploring every inch of her body with hungry, all-male dominance. And his voice, that honeyed, sexy voice of his, telling her he loved her. Lies, every word of it...

She made a rough, self-denigrating sound at the back of her throat, headed for her small bathroom and took a shower. She wouldn't think about him again. She would not. No need. He'd bought the painting that had brought him briefly back into her life and today it would be crated and dispatched. End of story.

The morning was just pleasantly hectic, leaving no room for brooding over those erotic dreams and she made time to accept Michael's invitation to lunch. The new, much publicised restaurant lived up to expectations as far as the food went but the service was slow.

'I don't know about you, but I'd better be getting back,' she declined when he suggested coffee to round off the meal. She was on the point of rising but he reached out and clasped her wrist.

'We're already late, a few more minutes won't make much difference. Besides, there's something I want to say to you.'

From the look in his eyes, the softening of his mouth, she knew what it was. And she didn't want to hear it. She wasn't ready.

His hand slid down to capture her fingers. 'You must know I'm attracted to you,' he said quickly. 'We already have a good relationship and I want to take it further. I don't know what you think about me, and I won't put you on the spot by asking, but you're all I admire in a woman. I'm pretty sure we could build something good and lasting together. You might not think so right now, but will you give it a try?'

Carefully, she slid her fingers away from his. What to say? Only yesterday she'd caught herself listening to the ticking of her biological clock again, knowing her pleasant working relationship with her employer's son was on the point of developing into something deeper, balancing the prospect of a lonely old age against the warm, emotional security of having a husband and family.

Yesterday she would have been comfortable with what he'd just said, agreed to go with the flow, find out if they would make a compatible couple.

So why the hesitation? What had changed? Something had.

'You don't fancy me at all?' he muttered into the suddenly spiky silence.

She smiled at him. He looked like a sulky child.

'I've never thought about it,' she said soothingly, lying smoothly to cover the lack of enthusiasm that was obviously upsetting him.

'But you will?' He made it sound like an order. 'Why not have dinner with me tonight? Since Justine left me I've learned to cook a mean steak. But, if you prefer, I could rise to beans on toast. Take your pick.'

His sudden, boyish grin gave her pause. She didn't know why his marriage had broken down after only a couple of years. Edward had voiced the general opinion that it was a blessing there were no children but apart from that he'd said nothing about the cause.

Whatever, Michael didn't deserve to be hurt again. She said with rare impulsiveness, 'I'm allergic to beans! Make it Monday, shall we, after the viewing!' She stood up, hitching the strap of her bag over her shoulder. 'One condition, though,' she warned. 'Friends. Nothing more, not yet. Nothing personal, Mike. I'm simply not ready for commitment.'

Not ready? When for weeks she'd often caught herself brooding about her long-term future. Children. Happy, family life. Not that she knew much about that…

'Condition accepted.' He stood up too, leaving

folded notes to cover the bill. 'But don't blame me if I try to change your mind. Eventually.'

She knew she'd made a mistake when she caught his satisfied smirk. Lunch was fine, but supper at his flat near the Barbican?

Misgivings shuddered through her. A week ago she would have seen the invitation as a natural progression of their deepening comradeship, would have pleasantly anticipated getting to know him on his home ground. Now she'd accepted his invitation because he was her friend, a nice guy, and she hadn't wanted to upset him with an outright refusal.

Back at the gallery there was a message for her at the front desk. Edward wanted to see her. Now.

Enclosed in the silver capsule that whisked her directly into Edward's office she filed the problem with Michael away at the back of her mind. She'd handle it as smoothly as she'd learned to handle everything else since she'd left the parental home at eighteen.

Handled everything except—

'Ben Dexter,' Edward said as the lift doors closed behind her. 'He needs you to appraise the contents of a property his company—or one of them—acquired relatively recently. About eighteen months ago, if I remember correctly.'

He arranged a few papers into a neat pile and then tapped it with the ends of his long, thin fingers, tilting his silver-grey head he asked, 'Are you unwell? You look a bit green around the gills—lunch upset you? Do please sit down.'

The shock of hearing that name slotted into her uncomfortable thoughts had driven what colour she did have out of her skin. It had nothing to do with what she'd eaten at lunch or her unfathomable change of attitude over her relationship with his son.

Besides, what company was Edward talking about? From what she knew of Dexter it was probably dodgy. Should she warn her boss, confess she knew Dexter to be a cheat and a liar? It was something to think about.

'I'm absolutely fine,' she claimed, gathering herself, slipping into the chair on the opposite side of his desk. 'You were saying?'

She wouldn't do it. If he wanted bits and pieces of antiques, paintings, whatever, appraised then someone else would have to do it. Her stomach churned over at the very thought of having to have anything at all to do with him.

Edward gave her a long look and then, as if satisfied, told her, 'His company, Country Estates, bought up this run-down house and land in Shropshire. They've sorted out the business end—planning permission for a golf course, clubhouse and leisure centre and a small heritage farm, and now they're turning their attention to the house itself.'

Caroline felt the shock of that like a physical blow. There could be few people who hadn't heard of the ultra-successful Country Estates, admired by big business and the environmental lobby alike. She must have misjudged him, having believed him to have obtained his wealth by nefarious means. The thought wasn't comforting. The idea of Ben Dexter as a liar, cheat and betrayer had been with her for so long that having to rethink it was like an amputation.

But what place were they talking about here? Suddenly she was sure she knew. Had Dexter's company acquired more than one run-down estate in Shropshire around eighteen months ago? It was possible, of course, but not very likely.

'Are we talking about Langley Hayes?' The smile she manufactured was just right. Borderline interested. Only she knew how heavily her heart was pounding.

'You know it?''

The slightest nod would do. She'd been born there, had lived there—apart from when she'd been away at boarding school—until she'd been driven out by misery and one dictate too many from her authoritarian father.

Of her mother she had no memory. Laura Harvey had died shortly after giving birth to Caroline. Only the occasional photograph in a barely opened album had shown her just how beautiful her mother had been.

She had never been back. She'd been warned not to show her face again. Attending her father's funeral out of duty, Caroline had not gone back to the house. It and the land had been sold to Country Estates, the bulk of the purchase price repaying the mortgage her father must have taken out on the property, the small residue going to Dorothy Skeet, his housekeeper, the woman who had also been his long-time mistress.

Apparently her non-commital nod had sufficed. Edward said, 'Dexter tells me the entire contents of the house were acquired at the time of the sale. Some of the things are fine, others definitely not. Though as he admitted, he's no expert. Which is why he wants you to do an appraisal.'

Careful, she told herself. Be very careful. Otherwise you might find yourself throwing your head back and howling out torrents of rage.

'This was discussed last night, after I left?' she asked levelly, crossing her long, elegant legs at the ankles, clasping her hands loosely together in her lap. They looked very pale against the dark sage of her tailored skirt. She knew what Dexter was doing—exactly what he was doing. And despised him for it.

'No, he phoned this morning. He left last night almost as soon as you did. It's been arranged that his driver will pick you up from your apartment at ten on Monday morning. I don't think you'll need to be away for more than three or four days. However, spend as much time there as it takes. Dexter's a client I'd like to hang onto.'

Just like that! 'It's my stint on the front desk next week, and with the extra work following a viewing I can't afford to be away,' she pointed out calmly.

All the qualified staff took it in turn to man the front. Hopeful people walked in off the street, carrying things in plastic bags or wrapped in newspapers, hoping to be told that granny's old jug or the painting they'd put up in the attic decades ago was worth a small fortune.

'Edna will cover for you at the front and, as for the rest, we'll cope without you. Dexter asked specifically for you, most probably because he'd already met you last evening.' He steepled his fingers, his eyes probing. 'Do I sense a certain reluctance?'

Too right! A deep reluctance to do Dexter's bidding, to let him pull her strings and put her in the position of sorting through the detritus of Reginald Harvey's life. It wasn't enough that the wild, penniless lad from the wrong side of the tracks who'd broken hearts with about as much compunction as he would break eggs, had bought up the lord of the manor's property—he wanted to put her, Caroline, in the position of humble retainer.

He wanted to turn the tables.

'Only in as much as it affects my work here.' She couldn't tell him the truth. She had shut her troubled past away years ago and refused to bring it out for anyone now.

'It won't. You're my right-hand man, but no one's indispensable.'

'Of course not,' she conceded, her smile too tight. She could refuse to go, and earn herself a big black mark. Edward was a wonderful employer but cross him and he'd never forgive or forget. She'd seen it happen. Resigned now, hoping Dexter wouldn't be at Langley Hayes, but prepared for the worst, she half left her seat but resumed it again, asking, 'I gather Dexter has personal financial clout? The price he paid for the Lassoon wouldn't be counted as peanuts in anyone's book.'

Know your enemy, she thought. And Dexter was hers. Leaving aside the way he'd treated her in the past, there was something going on here, some dark undercurrent. She felt it in her bones.

Edward could have refused to discuss his client but thankfully he seemed happy to do so. 'His cheque won't bounce,' he said drily. 'Rich as Croesus apparently. Came from nothing.' His smile was tinged with admiration. 'That's according to the only article I've ever read about him—financial press a year or so ago. He built a computer-software empire and is reckoned to be some kind of genius in the field. That's rock solid and growing, but he needed more challenges. That was when he diversified into property and now he's reputed to be a billionaire.'

'And he never even got close to being married?' She could have kicked herself for the unguarded remark. It wasn't like her. Her descent into what her boss would term idle tittle-tattle shamed her and Edward's displeasure was contained in his dismissive, 'I know nothing about the man's personal life.'

Taking her cue, Caroline rose, smoothed down her skirt and collected her bag. Back to business, she asked, 'Do you know whether or not he intends to dispose of anything of value?' There had been some lovely things she remembered. Although if her father had been in financial difficulty he might have sold them.

'From what I could gather he aims to keep the best

in situ. It will be up to you to report on what could be kept as an investment.' He began to shuffle the small pile of papers, a clear indication that her presence was no longer required.

Caroline left, wondering why the unknown details of Dexter's private life were like a burning ache in the forefront of her mind.

That Langley Hayes was in the process of restoration was not in doubt, Caroline thought as the driver parked the Lexus on the sweep of gravel in front of the main door. Scaffolding festooned the early-Georgian façade. The parkland through which they'd approached the house—unkempt in her own recollection—had been smoothly manicured and, in the middle distance, she'd seen two men working with a theodolite.

Surveying the land for the golf course? The clubhouse? The—what was it—leisure centre? Whatever, it was no longer any concern of hers. Her life here, largely lonely, hadn't been a bed of roses. She felt no pangs of nostalgia or loss. Only that nagging internal anxiety—would Dexter be here?

'A lot of work in progress,' she remarked, as she stood on the forecourt in the warm April sun as the driver opened the boot to collect her baggage, saying the first thing that came to mind to smother all those uncharacteristic internal flutterings.

'Mostly finished on the main house,' he answered, closing the boot. 'Structurally, anyhow.' His bushy eyebrows rose a fraction. 'You should have seen the state it was in. But the boss got everything moving—once he makes his mind up to something he don't hang about.'

He lifted her bags. 'If you'll follow me, miss, I'll rouse the housekeeper for you—Ms Penny. She'll look after you.'

The rows of pedimented windows gleamed as they had never done when she'd lived here and the main door had been newly painted. So Mrs Skeet hadn't been kept on, she pondered as she entered the spacious hallway. Ben Dexter obviously believed in making a clean sweep. His restlessness would push him towards the principle of out with the old and in with the new. And that went for his women, too, she thought with a stab of bitterness that alarmed her.

There had been no other car parked on the forecourt. Just the builder's lorry and a giant skip. Which didn't mean to say that his vehicle wasn't tucked away in the old stable block.

She asked, trying to ignore the tightness in her throat, the peculiar rolling sensation in her stomach, 'Is Mr Dexter here?' And held her breath.

'Couldn't say, miss. I generally take my orders from his PA. I'm just the driver. Now...' he set the cases down '...if you'll wait half a tick I'll go find Ms Penny.'

Caroline closed her eyes as she expelled her breath and slowly opened them again to take stock. The central, sweeping staircase had been freshly waxed, as had the linen-fold wall panelling. And the black and white slabs beneath her feet gleamed with care.

All vastly different from the dingy, increasingly neglected house she had been brought up in.

But echoes of the past remained. If she listened hard enough she could hear her father's acid voice. 'You will do as I say, Caroline, exactly as I say.' And even worse, 'I will not tolerate it. Village children are not suitable playmates. If you disobey me again you will be severely punished.' And Mrs Skeet's voice, pleading, 'Don't cross your dad, young Carrie. You know it isn't worth it.'

Her full mouth tightened. She had crossed him in the end. Monumentally. Had been forbidden the house. And had been glad to go, the legacy her mother had bequeathed her enabling her to continue her studies.

Might things have been different if her mother had lived? If she'd been the son her father had wanted?

'So you swallowed your Harvey pride. I more than half expected you to refuse to turn up.'

The soft dark voice punched through her like a body-blow. Her breath tensed and trembled in her lungs as she turned reluctantly to face him. He had entered by the main door behind her and although the hall was large by any standards he dominated it.

Gypsy-dark black eyes hinting at a wildness only superficially tamed, soft black hair fingered by the breeze, lithe body clothed in black, of course, to match his soul, snug-fitting jeans, topped by a fluid fine-cotton shirt.

Her heart stung deep in her breast. But she could hold her own. No longer in thrall to his seductive magic she was his equal, or more than, and not his willing toy.

The possibility that he might be here had had her dressing for effect, making a statement. Beautifully tailored, sleek deep blue suit, high-heeled pumps, her hair coiled into a knot at her nape, her stockings sheer and disgracefully expensive, her only jewellery a thin gold chain that shone softly against the milky-pearl skin of her throat. Where, to her deep annoyance, a pulse had started to beat much too rapidly.

'Where my work's concerned I have no prejudices. You hired a professional, Mr Dexter.'

'So I see.' A hint of amusement tugged at the corners of his long, sensual mouth as his dark eyes swept from the top of her glossy black hair to the tips of her shoes and back again to lock with hers. 'Such elegant packaging—exquisitely understated of course—such control. Every inch the daughter of the landed gentry.' His voice deepened to a honeyed drawl. 'I recall times when—'

'Mr Dexter.' She cut in firmly, desperately trying to ignore the way his lazy, explicit appraisal had set her skin on fire, had made the blood fizz alarmingly in her veins. 'Might I suggest we stick to why I'm here?' She broke off, sheer relief making her feel light-headed as a woman in her early thirties walked briskly towards them from the back of the house.

Short blonde hair curved crisply around an open, cheerful face, her short, wiry body clothed in serviceable blue jeans and a navy sweatshirt. Ms Penny? A far cry from the billowy, faded prettiness of Dorothy Skeet.

'Sorry to have kept you; Martin couldn't find me. Unblocking a drain.' Brisk voice but a warm smile. 'Lunch in fifteen minutes, boss. Breakfast room.' Bright grey eyes were turned on Caroline. 'I'll show you where you'll sleep, Miss Harvey.' She picked up the luggage and headed for the stairs.

Caroline followed, still light-headed enough to have to hold onto the banisters. It was bad enough that Dexter was around when he didn't need to be. She could have done the job she'd been hired to do without having him under her feet.

But if he was going to try to dredge up the past, make pointed comments on the way she looked then the next two or three days would be intolerable.

CHAPTER THREE

'HERE we go, then.' The housekeeper pushed open a door at the far end of the corridor that ran the full and impressive length of the house. 'No *en suite*, I'm afraid, but there's a bathroom next door.'

Caroline sucked in a sharp breath as she stood on the threshold. Was it coincidence or had Dexter issued instructions that she should be given this particular room?

He knew it had been hers. How many times had he tossed pebbles at the window to wake her? Countless. But she'd never been sleeping; she'd been waiting for his signal, full of longing for the arms of her secret lover, racked with anxiety in case he didn't come, ready to fly silently down the stairs to be with him, to melt with him into the magical beauty of the soft summer night.

A wave of ice washed through her, followed by unstoppable drenching heat. She shook her head, annoyed by her body's reaction, then firmed her mouth, a flicker of scorn darkening the deep blue of her eyes. She was too strong now to let him get to her on any level. In any event, the atmosphere of the room felt entirely different.

The faded nursery paper had been replaced by soft primrose-yellow emulsion and there was a pale ferny-green carpet instead of the cracked linoleum that had shrivelled her bare feet in wintertime—

'You'll have lunch with the boss—the breakfast room's the third door on the left, off the hall.' The housekeeper put the bags down at the side of the bed. 'He'll give you instructions on what he wants you to do, of course. But if there's anything else you need, you just let me know.'

'Thank you. It's Ms Penny, isn't it?'

Really, she had to get a grip, not go to pieces simply because she'd be using her old room for a night or two. She made herself smile, walk through the door instead of hovering like someone being urged to enter a chamber of horrors! For pity's sake, she didn't have to remember if she didn't want to!

'Call me Linda. I only come over Ms-ish when I'm on my dignity!' A disarming grin then a square, capable hand was extended and was taken.

'And I'm Caroline. Tell me, is Mr Dexter staying too, or is this a flying visit?' She hoped it was the latter, but she wouldn't put money on it.

'Staying, as far as I know. He comes and goes. Usually he just drops by from time to time to keep an eye on work in progress. But this time he arrived with a heap of luggage. Now...' a quick glance at the man-sized watch she wore '...I'll get lunch on the table. It's cold; I'm not much of a hand when it comes to cooking. Admin's my line and there won't be a cook in residence for another month, so you're going to have to take pot luck, I'm afraid.'

A live-in cook as well as a housekeeper to ensure

the smooth day-to-day running of the house. Dexter must have decided to make Langley Hayes his permanent home she mused as Linda left the room. Showing that the wild, penniless youngster could lord it over the village just as her father had done? Only in better style, with far more money to throw around.

Sucking her lower lip between her teeth Caroline methodically began to unpack. In a way she couldn't blame Dexter for what he was doing. Brought up by his mother—a rather fearsome woman, she remembered—paying a small rent for the dubious delights of living in a near derelict cottage on her father's estate which no one else would dream of inhabiting, the unconventional pair had been looked down on by the majority of the villagers. It would take a strong-minded man to resist the temptation to come back and display his new-found affluence.

Not that his motives interested her, of course. They didn't. Her only concern was getting the job done and getting back to London.

Aware of the passage of time, she squashed the childish impulse to refuse to go down to lunch at all. Refusing to face problems wasn't her style.

And he was a problem, she admitted as she opened the breakfast-room door a few minutes later. He was waiting for her, his back to the tall window that framed a view of newly manicured parkland. Tall, tough, beautifully built, even more compellingly handsome than he had been twelve years ago.

But there was something missing. There was no

sign of the former tenderness, or the sexily inviting smile that had captivated her, had bound her to him during that lost, lazy, loving summer. The man he had become was arrogant, his slight smile insolent, the dark glitter of his eyes speaking of derision overlaid with the bleak menace of an anger she couldn't understand. If anyone had the right to be angry it was she.

'So you decided not to ask for a tray in your room. Bravo!'

The nerve-pricking insolence deepened his smile. Caroline went very still. This had to stop, this needling. She opened her mouth to tell him as much but her lips remained parted and silent as he gestured with one finely boned, strong hand, 'Shall we eat?'

The small circular table had been haphazardly set with earthenware plates of cold-cut roasts and uninspired salads. But there was wine, an excellent muscat, she noted as she reluctantly took her place, vowing not to touch a drop. She needed to keep a clear head when dealing with the man who carried such an aura of danger.

She shivered suddenly and if she'd hoped she could keep that betraying reaction to herself she was doomed to disappointment.

'Cold?' An upwards twitch of one straight black brow. 'I thought it was unseasonably warm for mid-April.' He lifted the wine from the ice bucket, but she quickly placed her hand over her glass.

'No?' He poured sparingly for himself, his movements deft, undeniably pleasing. 'Then do help yourself—I think we've been given beef.' A semi-humorous glance at her pale, set features. 'And I apologise for the cheap plates and cutlery. But that's the way the cookie crumbles. Your father must have sold all the family silver along with the Royal Worcester.'

They'd eaten from Minton, not Worcester, the pieces mismatched but beautiful, the silver flatware heavy, with richly decorated handles. She felt colour stain the skin that covered her cheekbones.

'Cut it out!' she ground out unthinkingly, her lips tightening at his undisguised taunt. She hadn't meant to rise, had decided to ignore any sly jibes coming from him, but it hadn't happened; she hadn't been able to help herself.

Her hands knotted together in her lap, she added heatedly, 'I know why you wanted me to come here, so let's take it as read, shall we? Then perhaps I can get on with the work you hired me for.'

The urge to get to her feet and walk out of this room was strong. But she wouldn't do it; it would be another display of regrettable temperament, letting him know just how easily he could get to her.

So she sat mutinously still, hoping her features displayed nothing but boredom now. Until he leant back, one arm looping over the back of his chair, lazy mockery in his dark velvet voice.

'So you tell me—why did I want you here?'

Anger kicked inside her again and she said goodbye to all her remaining control for the first time in years, huge, thickly lashed violet eyes snapping as they clashed with the black enigma of his. 'Because my father called you the scum of the earth.' She recalled his exact words, spoken contemptuously so long ago. 'You stole from him, you were a danger to the morals of the village girls—'

That didn't hurt her, not now, not after so many years! How could it?

'You lived in squalor. So when father died, in debt, and you were able to buy up his property, you decided to drag me here and rub my nose in it!'

Suddenly running out of steam she sagged back. Since his callous betrayal of her younger self she'd learned not to have strong emotions, certainly not blind, unthinking anger. Still, she supposed, it was better said than not. Bottled anger festered, left scars.

'Wrong,' he said lightly, his long mouth twitching unforgivably, her tirade and character assassination not causing him a moment's discomfiture. 'But interesting. My mother and I lived in squalor because when we arrived in the village we couldn't afford anything else and it gave your father a very small income while the cottage was in the process of falling down.

'And as for stealing from him...' long fingers played with the stem of his wine glass, the dark, hypnotic depths of his eyes holding hers '...I was fourteen when we came here and was under the mistaken impression that the trout in the stream that ran behind our hovel were free for the taking. Your father put me right with the aid of a rather threatening shotgun.

'That said...' his mouth hardened '...I didn't bring you here to rub your disdainful little nose in my financial success. Your presence here is a necessity.'

'Now,' he inserted coolly, handing her the platter of cold meat, 'I suggest we eat, and then you can get down to work.'

Once, he'd told her she was necessary to his happiness; now, her expertise was the only thing he wanted from her. She swallowed convulsively, wishing her mind didn't stray into the past, comparing it to the uncomfortable present. Another impulse came to cut and run. But Edward would not be pleased, and that was putting it mildly. Dexter was paying handsomely for her presence here. Walk out and the gallery would lose a potentially valuable client, acquire a black mark against its venerable name.

Grimly, she speared a slice of beef, added a tomato and wondered if she'd be able to force any of it down. He hadn't countered the claim that he'd been a moral danger to the village girls simply because he couldn't.

Did he know he'd left at least one fatherless child behind him when he'd disappeared from the village, richer by the several hundred pounds her father had paid him to leave, an amount that must have seemed like a fortune to him back then? Of course he did. Maggie Pope had told him her baby daughter was his. He hadn't wanted to know.

'As I'm here to sort out the dross from the remaining good pieces, perhaps you would tell me where you'd like me to start. Or do I have a free hand?'

She did her best to sound brisk and business-like, to put the regrettable disturbance of the personal behind her. But recalling the part of her life that had left her disillusioned, hurt and betrayed had sapped her energy, had made her feel drained.

She was hardly in a fit condition to endure the long appraisal he gave her expensively tailored, slim jacket, the fine fabric and sophisticated style discreetly announcing a coveted designer label before he stated, 'Start at the top and work down. I don't think the contents of the attics have been looked at in years. And, I'll warn you, you'll find a fair amount of builders' rubble—part of the roof had to be retiled—among the dust and grime of decades. It can be properly cleaned out once you've decided if there's anything up there worth keeping.'

He finished the wine in his glass and said with a flicker of impatience, 'If you've finished mangling your food perhaps you would make a start.'

He was vile! Caroline thought as she stood in the open attic doorway. He had looked at the way she was dressed and had deliberately sent her up here.

It was even worse than she'd remembered, lumps of fallen, crumbling plaster littered the cobweb-shrouded disintegrating boxes, weighed down the laughably named ragged and torn dust-sheets that only partly covered old, unwanted bits of furniture.

She had removed her stockings and replaced the

high heels with Gucci loafers but they, and her suit, would be ruined.

Had he guessed that the things she'd brought with her were all beautiful and expensive, that she'd been determined that if he should show up he would see a cool, elegantly sophisticated career woman—in direct contrast to the wild, uninhibited young thing she had been when he'd held her in his arms, had made love to her, whispering of his adoration.

How he had changed! But, there again, maybe he hadn't. That streak of cruelty had been inherent in his nature. He couldn't have used and betrayed her, lied to her, if it hadn't. Or abandoned the woman who had given birth to his child.

She turned abruptly on her heels and backtracked down the twisty attic staircase. Linda was at the kitchen table, making notes in a ledger.

Taking in the new quarry-tiled floor, the huge state-of-the-art cooking range, immense dishwasher and commercial-sized fridge, Caroline wondered briefly if Dexter intended to settle down to marriage, raise an enormous family, then dismissed that from her mind as something of no consequence and asked, 'Do you have an overall I could borrow? I've been asked to clear out the attics.'

'Oh lord, they're filthy, aren't they?' Linda laid down her pen and gave her a sympathetic smile as she got to her feet. 'I said the whole lot should be put on a bonfire, but the boss said there might be something of sentimental value. Apparently, this house was owned by some monumental old snob—

been in the family for generations. He's dead now, but there was a daughter. The boss said to leave it as it was. She might come back some time and be gutted if she found family stuff had been destroyed.'

Had Dexter really been that thoughtful? Something twisted sharply inside her. Had he really believed she might return at some time in the future? Had he taken his opportunity to force her to return to the family home when they'd eventually met up again because he wanted her to have anything of sentimental value?

And where did that leave her theory that his prime motivation was to turn the tables on her?

But she was too shaken by what she'd heard to try to work out his motives. She said heavily, 'Then, he can't have sent me to work in the attics solely because he wanted to see me get my hands dirty. I am the daughter of that monumental old snob.'

A heartbeat of silence. Linda gave her a startled look. 'I'm sorry. I had no idea—'

'Don't worry about it. He was an incurable snob. He believed he had a position to uphold, but the problem was he didn't have the wherewithal to sustain it.'

That had been common knowledge, he hadn't known that the people from the village had laughed at him behind his back. She didn't add that he'd been authoritarian, cold and unloving. He had been her father, after all. She owed his memory some loyalty.

'I—well—' Linda was clearly embarrassed by her *faux pas*. 'I don't go in for overalls, but I think the previous housekeeper left some behind. Hang on a tick, I'll see what I can find in the box of stuff put out for the next jumble sale.'

Moments later she was back carrying a small pile of laundered, folded garments. Flimsy nylon, flower-patterned overalls. Very feminine, very Mrs Skeet.

'Do you know where Mrs Skeet is now?' Curiosity and a slight, lingering affection for the woman who had looked after her—in a fashion—prompted Caroline to ask as she tucked the overalls under her arm.

'Rents the cottage next to the village stores,' Linda supplied. 'When the renovation work started here she came up two or three times to clear out your father's clothes. Nice woman, a bit prone to flap. You could tell she was gutted by your old man's death.'

The question, Why hadn't his daughter undertaken that sombre task? lurked at the back of the other woman's eyes but Caroline wasn't answering it. 'I'll make time, one evening while I'm here, to visit her.' Her accompanying smile was small and social as she turned and walked away. She knew why her father had forbidden her the house, had said he never wanted to see her again. But she would never know why he had been unable to feel any affection for her at all. Maybe Dorothy Skeet could supply the answer.

Caroline hung up her suit and buttoned one of the overalls over her black satin bra and briefs. The skimpy fabric was virtually transparent and the splashy blue and pink roses were a nightmare. Plus, the thing itself was oceans too large.

Not to worry that she looked completely ridiculous; no one would see her and her suit would be saved from certain ruination.

Back in the airless space beneath the roof she began to work methodically, clearing an area at one end where she could stack rubbish, hauling boxes of chipped china and battered saucepans, a collapsed Victorian whatnot, over the uneven, dusty boards, wondering why people hoarded useless objects, then remembering how in her childhood she had found magic up here, the perfect antidote to many a wet and lonely day.

There had been a dressing-up box, at least that was how she'd thought of it: A tin trunk full of old clothes, probably once belonging to her great-grandmother and her mother, most of the things beautiful and all of them fragile. Period dresses could fetch big money, especially if they were in good condition and, remembering back, most of them had been.

After some searching she found the trunk, lifted the lid and found it empty, apart from a bundle of letters tied up with faded ribbon. Her father must have sold the things when money got tight. At Dorothy Skeet's prompting? She could remember the housekeeper's voice as if it was yesterday, 'I thought I'd find you up here. It's time for bed. And mind what you're doing with those things—they can be really valuable. Still, if dressing up keeps you quiet and out of the way—'

Caroline sank down on her heels. Her shiny black

hair had come adrift from its moorings. She pushed it back off her face with a dusty hand, leaving a dark smudge on the side of her milky-pale face.

If only her father could have swallowed his pride and sold Langley Hayes instead of re-mortgaging it, moved to a much smaller place, then he could have spent his final years free from financial worry. But his sense of self-importance wouldn't have let him do that.

Sighing, she reached for the letters. They were from her father, written to her mother before their marriage. She selected the one at the top of the bundle and began to read. A few lines were enough to tell her that they'd been deeply in love with each other, a few more told her that the young Reginald Harvey had adored and worshipped his beautiful bride-to-be.

She slipped the letter back in its envelope and bound it back with the others, her fingers shaking. This was personal and private and showed her a side of her father she had never known existed. He had been capable of a love so strong and enduring it practically sang from the faded pages.

Clutching the letters, she got to her feet, her eyes blurred with sudden tears. And saw him. She couldn't breathe.

She hadn't given Ben Dexter a single thought for the last couple of hours but now he was standing in the open attic doorway, watching her. And he filled her head, the whole drowsy, dusty space. The atmosphere was charged with his presence.

If she'd explained to her father— the thought came fleetingly—just how deeply she'd been in love with Ben Dexter instead of stubbornly remaining mute, her eyes defiant, then perhaps he would have understood. He had known the type of love that could enthral, that could bind one person to another with a special kind of magic.

Just as swiftly that thought was replaced by something much more cynical: it wouldn't have made a blind bit of difference. Even if her father could have been persuaded to approve of her relationship with the village wild boy instead of threatening fire and brimstone there wouldn't have been a happy ending. The black-eyed, half tamed, young Dexter had never loved her. Had just lied about it because he'd wanted sex with her, happy enough to go find it elsewhere when he'd had a fistful of her father's money as a pay-off.

Now the downward sweep of his eyes, the curl of his long, hard mouth told her that he'd noted her weird appearance and had fastened on what was obvious: the clear outline of her svelte body showing through the ghastly overall, modesty secured, but only just, by the tiny black bra and briefs.

Quelling the impulse to run right out of here, she lifted her chin a fraction higher and coolly asked, 'You wanted something?'

'You.'

Eyes like molten jet swept up and locked with hers and for a moment she thought he meant it. Meant just that. Her bones trembled, heat fizzing through her veins, her breath lodging in her throat. Until a deep cleft slashed between his dark brows, the lazy, taunting smile wiped away as he moved closer.

Of course he hadn't meant he wanted her the way he once had. Wildly, passionately, possessively. He just wanted to check the hired help was actually working, not sitting somewhere with her feet up, painting her nails.

Which was just as well because she didn't want him, most certainly she didn't. Until he touched her, the merest brush of the backs of his fingers as he stroked the heavy fall of midnight hair away from her face and everything inside her melted in the shattering conflagration of present desire and remembered ecstasy.

Dry-mouthed, she could hardly breathe, the air tasting thick and heavy on her tongue as he touched the wet spikiness of her lashes with the tip of his forefinger and said heavily, 'You're upset, Caro. I didn't mean that to happen, I truly didn't.'

Concern in those black, black eyes, a bone-melting softness. She remembered how that look could slice straight into her heart. Remembered that time, all those summers ago, a moonlit night, she'd collided with a sapling oak because when she'd been with him she'd seen nothing else. The same look as then, as he'd stroked the soft white skin of her shoulder, as if his touch, his love, could have stopped the slight abrasion from hurting, prevented a bruise from forming. She hadn't doubted the sincerity of his concern for her then.

But she should have done.

'I thought there might be something here of sentimental value,' he told her softly. 'Souvenirs of your childhood, photograph albums, whatever; things you might like to keep. Mrs Skeet has your father's personal effects. I know she intended to contact you. I'll arrange for the two of you to meet up while you're here.'

His hand lay lightly on her shoulder and her whole body tightened in rejection of what he was now and what he had been. Unwittingly, her eyes came up and levelled on his mouth. It looked as if he'd kissed more women than he'd had hot dinners. And as a well-worn cliché it probably hit the mark.

'No need,' she answered, keeping her voice steady, hard, even. 'I'd already decided to contact Dorothy. So far...' she shrugged his hand away '...I've found nothing of any value or interest apart from these letters which I intend to keep. But I'll continue looking.'

Oh, how she wished she didn't look so darned ridiculous! That Dorothy's cast-off overalls had been made from good, solid cotton, something, anything, that didn't reveal her skimpy underwear to eyes that were now hard, definitely ungiving. Because she'd rejected his concern as certainly as if she'd physically pushed the words back down his throat?

'Not now.' He turned away from her. 'Carry on in the morning. I told Linda we'd eat out this evening; she's got enough on her hands without having to feed us.' He paused in the doorway, turned to look at her, his voice hovering between frustration and amusement, 'Change out of that whatever it is—nightdress?—and be ready to leave in thirty minutes.'

CHAPTER FOUR

'I'M SURE you must be hungry by now. You barely touched your lunch.' No hint of that deeply unsettling caring in his voice now, just a smoky curl of amusement.

It was eight o'clock and the light was beginning to fade from the clear, evening sky. His teeth gleamed whitely against the olive tones of his skin as he switched off the ignition and gave her the self-assured, chillingly predatory smile that sent a rapid succession of shivers down the length of her spine.

She could have said with truth that she was absolutely ravenous, that it was his fault she hadn't been able to swallow more than a mouthful of her lunch. But she gave a brief dip of her glossy dark head and told him, 'Slightly,' instead.

Expecting the village pub she'd dressed as down as she could, given the selection of clothes she'd brought with her. But they'd ended up on the forecourt of what looked like a formidably exclusive eating house in the depths of the country and if the female clientele were all wearing little black numbers she'd stick out like a sore thumb in her cream linen trousers, toning Italian sweater and Gucci loafers.

Not that she was going to let it bother her, she decided as her assumption proved correct. In any case, Ben Dexter, immaculately suited, with his darkly virile looks, his obvious sophistication, stole all the attention. And sitting opposite him as they were handed menus as large and difficult to handle as broadsheets she wondered why he was bothering to try to impress her.

For the same reason he'd wanted to impress the locals when he'd bought the Langley Hayes estate—despised poor boy makes good?

He'd impressed her far more twelve years ago when he'd had two burning ambitions: To make her his wife and to achieve the financial success to keep her in style. At least, that was what he had said, and she'd believed him. Gullible fool that she'd been!

Oh, the success had come, no doubt about it, and she hadn't been interested in being kept in style—but as for making her his wife, nothing had been further from his lying, cheating mind.

She handed her menu to a passing waiter, glad to be rid of it. She said, lightly, coolly, 'I'll be a little late starting in the morning. I need to walk down to the village to see if Angie Brown still carries a stock of jeans and shirts. I need something serviceable if I'm going to spend half my time rooting around in the attics. And I was wearing one of Dorothy Skeet's overalls. I don't go to bed in billowing yards of flowery stuff.'

Suddenly the black eyes were laughing at her, his mouth a sinful curve, and she knew it had been a huge mistake to remind him that he'd suggested she was wearing her nightdress when he said, 'What do you wear to bed these days? Tailored silk pyjamas? There was a time when our bed was the softest, coolest moss we could find, if you remember. Or, if it rained, and it rarely did, the sweetly rustling hay in your father's stable loft. Neither of us wore a stitch back then.'

And then, without missing a beat, while thick hot colour swept into her cheeks and something nameless twisted viciously inside her, he said, 'The village store altered five years ago when Angie retired. The new owners don't stock clothing. But I need to drive into Shrewsbury tomorrow; you can come with me. You can shop while I keep my appointment with my solicitors.' He broke a bread roll with those long, strong fingers, buttered one ragged half and added softly, 'There's a rather good trattoria in Butcher Row. We can meet there for lunch.'

Just like that! Oh lord, let me get my composure back, she prayed, willing her pulse beat back to normal. Dropping explicit reminders of the past into everyday conversation was going to do her head in if he persisted. Best to ignore it. Hope it was a one-off.

'I would have thought you'd have used a firm of slick city lawyers.' She took up the conversational ball, ignoring his reference to the long, stolen nights they'd spent together, hoping that in future he would do the same. If he didn't then she'd be forced to have her say, and she didn't want to have a stand-up fight with him, risk him complaining to Edward, putting the job she loved in jeopardy. Much better to try to hold her tongue on the vexed subject of their past and keep their present relationship as businesslike as it was possible to be under the circumstances.

'No. I believe in supporting local firms—now.' As their waiter approached, he added, 'What will you have?'

She recited her order of Danish tartlets followed by red mullet with mushrooms abstractedly. By referring to himself as local he'd made it plain that he intended to settle at Langley Hayes. Being surrounded by his company's golf course and leisure centre would be a small price to pay for the self-aggrandisement of living in the home of his former enemy.

A home large enough to house a wife, a growing number of children and an army of servants. The thought that he might be contemplating marriage made her feel almost terminally ill.

Though it shouldn't. He was less than nothing to her now and she pitied his future wife. Once a liar and cheat, always a liar and cheat where women were concerned. She refused his offer of wine, ate well, made banal conversation and was thankful when they left.

The headlights made a sweeping golden tunnel beneath the newly leafing trees that overhung the narrow lane. Soon the Queen Anne's lace would foam on the verges and the wild roses and honeysuckle would bloom, filling the air with fragrance.

Her childhood had been lonely and often miserable

but even so she loved this part of the country. But her life was in London now, her home, her work, her friends. She didn't want or need to feel this utterly surprising, aching pang of nostalgia.

Without thinking, as they swept onto the driveway of Langley Hayes, she said tartly, 'I'm sure the area has a need for a golf course and leisure facilities—your company wouldn't have gone for it if they hadn't done their homework—but won't you mind being surrounded by people? Father would have had a fit if he'd found what he called the *hoi polloi* wandering around his property.'

'I'm not your father,' he observed coldly and she tightened her mouth in mute acknowledgement. He was far more handsome and charismatic than her father had ever been, worked hard—he must do to have acquired what was obviously a massive fortune where her father had lived on dwindling capital, and had mismanaged what had been left of the once enormous estate. But both men possessed a streak of cruelty, a complete disregard for other people's feelings.

'And I won't be here that often to be troubled by the masses,' he added sardonically. 'However, I will keep a suite of rooms here.'

He parked the gleaming Jaguar perilously close to the builder's skip, the tyres crunching on badly targeted lumps of plaster and brick ends. Caroline, getting out before he did, wondered if he was always as careless with his possessions as he was with other people's emotions.

She entered the house before he did but he caught up with her. 'Share a bottle of wine with me?'

His voice had lost that sharp edge and here in the soft silence of the house his presence was sensationally male and potent. And dangerous.

She shuddered inside. How easy it would be to give in to the temptation. Just be with him, get to know the man he had become. Wonder if he still made love as generously as he had done all those years ago or if he'd become jaded, taking his physical pleasure perfunctorily.

She slammed the door of her mind shut on that thought and shook her head slightly. 'Thank you, but I'll pass. What time do you leave for Shrewsbury tomorrow?'

'Ten. We should be back here by three. Are you sure about that wine?'

'Perfectly sure.' The best part of tomorrow would be wasted if she went with him. Spending more time with him than was absolutely necessary wasn't on her agenda. Why hadn't she had the foresight to bring something rough-and-ready to wear? Because none of her clothes fitted that category.

She smothered a sigh and said, 'I'll pass on the shopping trip, too. I'll manage with what I have.' Better to ruin her clothes than the image of a cool and collected professional. There was a limit to how much time she could spend with him without giving in to the temptation to tell him how much he disgusted her.

She turned her back and headed for the stairs and

heard him say softly, 'Running scared, Caro? I wonder why?'

In her room she closed the door and leant back against it, breathing heavily, her heart banging against her ribs. She felt as if she'd run a marathon with the devil on her tail. And the devil was Ben Dexter.

Once she'd adored him; he'd become her sole reason for living and her life had fallen apart when he'd betrayed her. But that betrayal didn't alter his incredible physical appeal. It should do, but it didn't.

She pushed herself away from the door, more than annoyed with herself for the direction her thoughts were taking. Furious.

Selecting an aqua silk nightdress and matching robe she went to the bathroom and ten minutes later, belting the robe around her narrow waist, she walked back and found Linda tapping on her bedroom door.

'I thought you might like to borrow these. They'll be too wide and too short, I guess, but they'll be more practical than those wispy flowery things.'

Caroline gave her heart-stopping smile. She could have hugged the other woman. She wouldn't have to ruin her own clothes and, more to the point, she wouldn't have to wonder when Dexter might walk in on her to make a point of looking at her underwear!

'Thanks, Linda!' She accepted the neatly folded jeans and faded green sweatshirt, debated whether to ask why Dexter, with the whole house at his disposal, would be keeping just a suite of rooms for his occasional use, and then thought better of it. Questions like that would only display an interest she desperately wanted to deny, particularly to herself. 'This is really thoughtful of you,' she said instead.

'Think nothing of it,' Linda gave a slight shrug, asking, 'Did you enjoy your evening?'

'The food was excellent.' She evaded the question, one hand going to the doorknob, turning it, opening the bedroom door. She didn't want to talk about it.

'Good.' Linda took her dismissal with an easy smile. 'I'll say goodbye in case I don't see you again. I've got the rest of the week off—family christening; my sister's first and I'm godmother—so you might have finished here before I get back.'

So she'd be alone here with Dexter, Caroline thought sinkingly as she smiled and said all the right things, and closed her bedroom door behind her telling herself staunchly that the other woman's absence wouldn't really matter. She could handle Ben Dexter all by herself; she didn't need backup.

He could no longer be remotely interested in her sexually. Been there, done that; his past history showed he was that kind of man. He had only insisted she come here so that he could demonstrate how well he'd done for himself, show her that he now had the upper hand.

Well, that she could handle, no problem; in fact she admired his financial acumen. As for the other, the unwanted sexual pull she was unable to hide from herself, well, she hated to admit it, but she was having difficulties.

And instead of being able to dismiss them from her wakeful mind she found herself lying in the darkness actually listening for his signal, the pebbles he'd lightly tossed against the window-pane, calling her down to him.

How willingly she'd gone…

She sat up, squirming to the edge of the bed, flicked on the bedside lamp and pressed her fingertips to her aching temples.

She had to pull herself together, stop remembering. They were different people now and she knew what a heartless bastard he really was. The man she'd loved all those years ago was nothing but a figment of her imagination, a silly romantic dream.

Her watch told her it was just gone two o'clock and she knew she wouldn't sleep. Why lie sleepless in bed, agonising over the past, when she could be working, bringing the time of her departure that little bit closer?

The decision made, she slipped her arms into the aqua silk robe once more, tied the belt securely and reached for her notebook.

She'd visit the dining room first she thought as she slipped silently down the great staircase. The Regency dining table with its twelve chairs had been sold long ago. She'd been about fourteen years old, home for the Christmas break and, when she'd questioned him, her father had said sarcastically, 'How else am I to pay your boarding school fees? Rob a bank? Ask the tooth fairy?'

Useless to tell him, for perhaps the fourth time,

that she'd have been happier at the nearest comprehensive. He'd given that withering look he'd seemed to reserve for her alone. 'Remember who you are!'

Who she was. Suddenly she had the unnerving feeling that she didn't know. A successful woman in her own right or a rootless shadow, pining for a lost love? Being back here with the boy who had been forbidden in the grounds, now transformed into a hard-eyed man who owned everything around her, made her feel unreal.

Shrugging off the unsettling feeling she turned her mind back to business. The table had gone, never replaced because her father had never entertained. But there had been a mahogany serving table—George III she thought—and a large dresser of around the same period. Both would be valuable and would represent a sound investment.

Pushing open the double doors and quietly closing them behind her she unerringly found the light switch and stood for a moment, transfixed by what she was seeing, wishing she had swallowed her distaste at seeming to be interested, and had asked Linda what plans Dexter had for the house.

The ugly, dark red flocked wallpaper had been stripped away, replaced by warm primrose-yellow emulsion. The boards beneath her feet gleamed and two refectory tables, complete with long bench seats, took up the centre of the room while comfortable but functional armchairs surrounded the huge fireplace.

Remembering the catering-size kitchen equipment, the extra, functional bathroom that had been made in what had once been a bedroom next to her own, she began to put two and two together. But a country house hotel didn't make real sense. Everything was too basic.

Hearing the double doors behind her open she stiffened, holding her breath, praying that it was Linda doing the investigating, not Dexter.

But her luck was out, as it always had been with him, and he walked into her line of vision, dressed in black, a soft V-necked sweater over well-worn jeans, his feet bare, as were hers.

Her heart thumped, a bolt of electricity zapping through her bloodstream. He looked so unfairly sexy, his dark hair rumpled, his jaw shadowed, his black eyes glinting beneath heavy, brooding lids. How well she remembered that look, the promise it offered—and delivered.

'You couldn't sleep? I wonder why,' he uttered silkily, his eyes sweeping the length of her body, lingering on the soft curves and hollows that the tightly belted, slithery robe did precious little to conceal. He made her so aware of how little she was wearing.

'Something I ate at dinner. Indigestion,' she lied, desperately trying to ignore the quivers of sexual response that were careering right through her. She didn't want this to happen to her, to feel anything for him other than utter contempt.

And, the pity of it was, no other man had ever had this effect on her. She'd dated, of course she had; she hadn't turned into a man-hater. But no one had ever come near to invoking the intense emotions, the devastating physical needs Ben had awoken within her.

The notebook she was holding shook in her hands. She made herself open it, remove the pen that was clipped inside the spiral of metal that bound it together, and said, 'As I couldn't get to sleep I thought I might as well do some work. I hadn't meant to disturb you.'

'Meant or not, you did. And do,' he responded drily. 'And did you? Work?'

Wildly, she cast her eyes round the room that was now so different from how she remembered it, gathered her scattered mental resources and said, 'There used to be a serving table. Father probably sold it, unless you've moved it somewhere else.'

'Nope.'

She wasn't looking at him but she had the distinct impression he'd moved closer. Much closer. Her skin prickled. She said, her voice thickening deplorably, 'The dresser's still here. Georgian. Valuable. Hang onto it if you're looking for an investment.'

'At the moment all I'm looking at is you.'

Caroline gulped, her breath fluttering in her throat. What he'd said was true. She could feel his eyes on her, burning her flesh. She wanted out of here. Now. But her legs wouldn't move. Then she felt his hand on her waist, searing through the fine layers of silk, sending flickers of fire to her pulse points, each and every one of them. Don't, she wanted to say. Don't touch me. But her tongue was cleaving to the roof of her mouth.

'You're cold; the central heating's turned down to the minimum. Let's go. Warm milk should settle your—indigestion.'

The pressure of his hand increased, she could feel the exact placement of every fingertip. Now was the time to tell him she didn't want his hot milk, or his manufactured concern, to take herself back to her room. But she didn't. She simply went where he led, appalling herself by her mindless regression to that summer all those years ago when she would have followed him to purgatory and back if he'd asked her to.

'You haven't asked why I found it impossible to sleep,' he said as they entered the warmth of the kitchen. 'Don't you think that would be the correct response in the course of polite conversation?'

The dark rub of irony in his voice touched a raw nerve. What lay between them precluded normal polite conversation. But then, she remembered, he'd always had beautiful manners, despite his wild ways, always seemingly highly tuned into the feelings of others.

Seemingly.

She said nothing, just hovered, her slender body as taut as a bowstring, watching as he poured milk into a pan and reached for two mugs, a bottle of brandy. She knew she should walk out of the room, break this strangely prickly intimacy but some dark compulsion kept her where she was, just as much in thrall to his male vitality, his smouldering sexuality as she had ever been.

'Then, I'll tell you, since you don't seem inclined to ask.'

The mere sound of his voice made her catch her breath, her teeth sinking into the soft flesh of her lower lip. If she'd had her wits about her she would have said, Don't bother, I'm not interested. But her wits had gone on holiday, along with her common sense.

And he told her, 'Thinking of you, sleeping under the same roof, wasn't conducive to a peaceful night's rest. I needed something to read to take my mind off it. That was when I saw the strip of light under the dining-room doors.' He shot her a brief, frowning glance. 'I thought it would be easy, but it isn't.'

He poured the hot milk into the two mugs and Caroline drew her fine brows together.

What wasn't easy? Having her around? Was his guilty conscience pricking him? Why didn't he say what he meant? He always had before. He'd had deep emotions and he'd expressed them freely, had been totally up front about what he'd wanted. Her.

Just for a time, she reminded herself tiredly. Another notch on his bedpost, the sheltered daughter of the local landowner who had treated him like scum, no less. How he must have been laughing at her father!

And how he had changed. Not an emotion in sight. A puzzling flicker of anger once in a while but nothing else. Watching him rinse out the milk pan and put it in the cavernous depths of the dishwasher she determined to get at least one straight answer out of him: an answer to the question that had been teasing her mind.

'What plans have you for this house?'

'Ah.' His smile was slightly cynical. 'I wondered when your curiosity would get the better of that aloof mantle you assume for me.' He picked up the steaming mugs. 'I suggest we drink this in the comfort of the library. And I'll tell you what I have in mind for Langley Hayes. And in return you can tell me what messed up your relationship with—what was his name?—the Honorable Jeremy Curtis, wasn't it? You were due to celebrate your engagement on your eighteenth birthday. Quite a catch for the only daughter of an impoverished local squire. So what went wrong? Did he find out you'd been enjoying a bit of rough trade and call it off? You must have been devastated, especially when you'd been so insistent that we keep our meetings so carefully secret.'

CHAPTER FIVE

CAROLINE couldn't believe he'd said that!

Almost tripping over herself in her rush to catch him up, she followed him to the library, a small book-lined room furnished with the scuffed old leather sofas that had been here for as long as she could remember.

He knew why they'd kept their affair secret, damn him! He knew what her father had been like! And how dared he imply that she'd been using him just for sex!

He'd made space for the mugs on the cluttered top of a low table and now bent to flick on the electric fire. Caroline watched him through narrowed eyes, biting back the scalding torrent of recriminations.

If he'd made that insulting remark twelve years ago she would have responded with passion, hitting out, probably biting and scratching too! But she was older now, a hell of a lot older and in total control.

The angry thump of her heart threatened to push a hole in her breastbone, but she picked up one of the mugs in both shaking hands and sank down into the corner of a sofa.

She was not going to let him see he could still reach her on any emotional level. No way. Unlike her younger self, she could control her reactions to whatever he did or said.

So, treating his insulting remark about rough trade with the contempt it deserved, she ignored it and said, her voice tight and hard with the effort of masking her angry emotions, 'Any engagement was in my father's head, and Jeremy's, not mine.'

'Really? An engagement was arranged without one side of the happy couple being aware of it?'

Plainly, he didn't believe her. He was standing a few paces away, facing her, a straddle-legged stance. The way he'd hooked his thumbs into the low-slung waistband of his jeans drew her riveted attention to the narrow span of his hips, his tautly muscled thighs.

She wrenched her eyes away, fastened them on the mug she was cradling in her hands and lifted it to her lips. A hefty swallow told her that his lacing of brandy had been far more than generous. Nevertheless, it did begin to take the sharp edge off her anger.

She pulled in a breath. For some no doubt nonsensical reason, she wanted him to believe her. What he thought of her shouldn't be important but on some deep, troubled level it was.

One more mouthful of the potent liquid, and then she explained tightly, 'Dad was at Oxford with Jeremy's father and they kept in touch. After all, they only live twenty-odd miles away. Dad was Jeremy's godfather and when I was young I used to spend school holidays with them. I think Lady Curtis thought I needed mothering, and Dad was glad to get me out from under his feet.

Then, when I was around thirteen, Lady C. was killed in a riding accident, and my visits stopped. But we still saw Jeremy. He and his father were about the only people we ever saw socially. Dad wanted me to marry him.'

She shrugged slightly, memories clouding her eyes. Marrying Jeremy, and the Curtis fortune, would have been the one and only thing she could have done to actually please her father.

'Was the poor devil in love with you?' Ben demanded. His voice was harsh, a strand of bitterness threading through the obvious scorn.

It was a question he had no right to ask. Besides, she didn't know the answer. Oh, she'd caught Jeremy looking at her in ways that had made her feel uncomfortable and she'd been the unwilling recipient of a couple of clumsy, slack-lipped kisses. But love—no, she didn't truly think so. Lust was more like it and a willingness to fulfil their respective fathers' wishes in that rather spineless way he'd had.

She merely shrugged, took another gulp of the brandy-spiked milk and widened her eyes in shock as he castigated abruptly, 'Still a heartless bitch!' Then his voice flattened, as if control had been sought and found, and he said, 'Your letter telling me my services were no longer required was obviously written a little too late. Because by then he must have found out that you'd been having some fun on the side and the engagement never took place. The man must have been gutted.'

He took a pace forward, bending to thrust his face close to hers, his black eyes brimming with contempt. 'And all you can do is shrug!'

Anger as hot and sharp as his pulsed through her. How dared he act this way! Putting her mug down on the faded Persian carpet she got to her feet, the tilt of her chin mutinous as she countered scathingly, 'You're trying to put the blame on me for what happened to hide your own guilt—it's what people do, isn't it? Why should you be any different?'

His dark eyes flared as he took a step towards her. Caroline stood her ground. The situation was explosive but she wasn't going to run away from it. He had been guilty of almost every sin in the book, not she!

The palms of her hands were slick with sweat and the heat of his body consumed her, as if the fire of their anger was pulling them closer instead of pushing them further apart.

His lips curled thinly in a parody of a smile. 'Is that so? Then you deny writing to tell me you never wanted to see me again? You didn't even do me the courtesy of telling me to my face.'

Of course she couldn't deny it! She wanted to hit him for trying to put her in the wrong. 'You weren't around.' She spat the words out scornfully. 'After my father had been to see you, you'd taken off, remember?'

Even now she could hear her father's thin, sarcastic voice, 'You can forget your loutish lover. I offered him money to make himself scarce, and he couldn't take it fast enough. He won't be back and, if that's not enough to cool your ardour, ask young Maggie Pope who fathered that brat of hers.'

Caroline expelled a shaky, emotional breath. She hadn't wanted this bitter confrontation, or the dreadful effect it was having on her body, making her aware of every pulse point, of every inch of burning, sensitised skin. The adrenalin flooding through her was turning passionate anger into a dark and dangerous pleasure.

'So I wrote you a letter and left it with your mother. What else did you expect?' she said, her voice a low, tortured growl.

She was out of here, she had to be, before she said something that would rob her of her pride, something that would tell him how much, and for how long, his cruel betrayal had affected her.

As if he'd read her intentions, Ben's hand curved sharply round the back of her neck, his black eyes burning into hers. 'What did I expect?' He repeated her words, his voice thick now. 'You tell me! But there was a time...' the fingers that had been like talons on her neck gentled with the suddenly lowered tone of his voice '...when you more than fulfilled all my wildest expectations. Remember?'

The soft, stroking movement of his fingers on her skin held her far more effectively than that earlier threatening grip. Sensations she had denied for so long were springing to demanding life, making her head spin giddily when he repeated thickly, 'Remember, Caro? Remember how we only had to look at each other? How looking was never enough? How we had to touch naked skin, move our bodies in the dance of love, how you couldn't wait to take me inside you?'

'Don't!' The word was a moan of denial, issued from quivering lips. Her whole body was shaking with all the old dark magic, uncomfortably mixed with the aching sense of loss and betrayal that still echoed through the years. 'Let me go,' she said thickly, her mind horrified by her body's sensual anticipation.

'I would if you wanted me to.' His voice purred softly. 'But you don't. You're as ready for me now as you ever were. Deny it all you like, but these don't lie...' Gently, he rubbed the ball of his thumb over her parted, pouting lips, the soft friction setting up a primal ache deep inside her, making her need to draw his thumb into her mouth take on a forbidden and self-destructive urgency.

He dropped his hand as if he'd read the need in her eyes, his fingers finding their way along the angle of her jaw, sliding down her throat and slipping beneath the edge of her robe where the soft silk trembled with the panicky force of the beats of her pulse.

'And neither do these,' he added, his voice slow, sultry, infinitely disturbing as long fingers grazed the crests of her blatantly peaking breasts, lingering, easing beneath the insubstantial barrier of fabric.

Caroline couldn't breathe. His caressing fingers

sent shafts of exquisite pleasure through her, just as they always had. Whatever he'd done in the past was obliterated for just this moment when the ties of passion were the only memories.

Her lips parting, she lifted her suddenly leaden eyelids and met the harsh, hungry lights in the narrowed blackness of his eyes. Her breath juddered on a soft whisper of sound, the atmosphere was so emotionally charged it stung—a million pinpricks of sexual awareness; sharp, intrusive, deeply exciting.

She could taste all the old need and raw desire on her tongue, here and now, not something left over from the past, sternly pushed away if it dared to float into her consciousness on the wings of memory. Here, binding her to him as it always had, here in the assured claim of his night-dark, compelling eyes, in the slight, slow smile that curved his undeniably beautiful mouth, a sizzlingly sexy smile that robbed her mind and body of all strength of character.

'So...' He expelled a long, slow breath, his thick lashes sweeping down as he gazed at her mouth. 'No denials, Caro?' His dark head bent, his mouth a breath away from hers. 'Good. That's good.'

Her lips parted in helpless invitation. She could smell the fresh almost savagely male scent of him; it made her giddy. And then his mouth touched the corner of hers and she turned her head, instinctively, urgently seeking the remembered heady magic of his kiss, that total surrender to the ecstatically wild passion that no other man had ever come near to making her feel.

But he merely touched her full lower lip with the tip of his tongue then lifted his head, both hands fastening lightly around her narrow waist, keeping his control where she had lost hers entirely, and she was almost sobbing with cruel frustration as he said wryly, 'Like taking candy from a baby.'

Ben released her, stepping back, his mouth compressed as his dark eyes swept over the evidence of her body's arousal, from her peaking breasts, her softened, parted lips, the haze of sexual desire that clouded her deep violet eyes. 'Round one to me, Caro,' he added, then jerked his head towards the door, his voice clipped, impersonal. 'Get some sleep. You'll need it. At seventeen you could be up all night and still look ravishing in the morning.' He gave a slight, humourless smile. 'But things change, don't they?'

The implication was that she would look like a raddled hag in the morning, that she was over the hill and, just as shaming, that she had lost everything that had once driven him to wild passion, unable to look at her without needing her with a desperation that had consumed them both.

How she managed to walk in a straight line, get out of the room, she didn't know. The humiliation was so intense it turned her bones to water and filled her head with a fiery red mist that blinded her.

When she woke Caroline was mildly surprised that she'd managed to sleep at all and not at all surprised to note the dark rings around her eyes. Her normally pearly translucent skin was grey and dull in the bright spring light that flooded the small bedroom.

No, she was no longer seventeen. His taunt came back to sting her. She was twenty-nine years old and should have known better than to let a deceitful, lying louse like Ben Dexter rouse her so effortlessly, rouse her to the point of being on the verge of pleading with him to make love to her.

A hot tide of shame raged through her, making her feel nauseous. Her own body had betrayed her as surely as he had done all those years ago.

She shook her head then pressed her fingers to her aching temples. So, OK, she thought wearily, she'd behaved like a fool, like the gullible teenager she'd been when she'd emerged from the cool canopy of the woods on that long-gone, hot summer afternoon to find Ben perched on the top of the drunken wooden gate that led to one of her father's neglected hay meadows.

He'd been wearing cut-off shabby denims and, apart from scuffed canvas deck shoes, nothing else. The skin that covered his whippy frame had been nut-brown, glistening, his dark unruly hair flopping over his forehead, his black eyes dancing with a million seductive lights, his smile dangerous and sexy as he'd dropped to his feet and had walked with slow deliberation towards her.

She'd felt it then, the sizzling chemistry; it had made her breathless, so she could barely answer when he'd said, 'So school's out. Something tells me it's going to be a great summer.' His eyes told her he liked what he saw, her slenderness cloaked in soft summer cotton, her black hair tumbling down to her waist.

She'd never been this close to him before. The effect was shattering. Of course she knew that he and his mother lived in the decrepit cottage down by the stream, had done for several years. And she'd seen him in the village once or twice and heard the mutterings about his wild ways. And she could understand them, the mutterings, almost sympathise with the staid village matrons because Ben Dexter was something else: too drop dead gorgeous, too charismatic. An untamed male.

All she could do was give him a wide smile of glorious recognition and take the hand he held out to her. And so it had begun…

Caroline gave a shaky sigh then tightened her lips. She'd been such a gullible fool then, and last night she'd have gone down the same path if Ben hadn't demonstrated that he wasn't remotely interested.

But it was no use brooding about it or wishing it hadn't happened. It had and she had to put it out of her head, salvage some pride, do her job and get out of here as quickly as she could.

A shower helped a little. No way was she going to dress in the old jeans and top Linda had lent her and scrabble around in the dusty attics. Today of all days she needed to have all flags flying, to retrieve some of her pride and somehow try to wipe away the shame.

Ben wouldn't be around to see what she looked like but she needed to look her best for her own sake.

Teaming the elegantly cut linen trousers she'd worn to the restaurant with an oyster silk shirt and a narrow tan belt she spent far longer than usual on her make-up, achieving a discreet and perfect mask. Then she fixed her glossy hair into her nape with a mock-tortoiseshell comb.

Linda was at the kitchen table, a sheet of paper in front of her. She got up, smiling, as Caroline entered. 'Good—I was just about to leave you a note; now I don't have to bother. There's cold stuff in the fridge and loads of tins in the wall cupboards. So help yourself. I guess the boss will do the same—he's already left for Shrewsbury… And don't tell me you're going to tackle the attics in that outfit! Didn't the jeans and top fit?'

'I'm sure they will.' Caroline followed her nose to the coffee pot. 'I thought I'd give the attics a miss today and make a start on the first floor.' She lifted the pot. 'Like some?'

Linda wrinkled her pert nose. 'Go on, then, twist my arm! I should be on my way, but another ten minutes won't make much difference.' She sat down again, watching as Caroline filled two mugs. 'Tell me, how do you manage to look so flippin' stylish? It's something you're born with, I guess. Me, I look all wrong whatever I wear!'

'I'm sure that's not true.' Caroline sat opposite the other woman and handed her the milk jug and sugar bowl. She felt really mean; Linda obviously wanted to settle into girl talk but she herself had other ideas.

Last night she'd fully intended to satisfy her now burning curiosity and ask Ben what his plans were for Langley Hayes. And now, after what had happened, she would make sure that she had as little to do with him as possible during the remainder of her time here. So that precluded any conversation longer than one syllable.

So before Linda could start talking about clothes and make-up she said, 'I can't help noticing that the house has a rather institutional look. Comfortable and much brighter than it ever was when I lived here—but functional. What does Mr Dexter intend to do with it?'

'Don't you know?' Linda widened her eyes then gave a wry smile. 'No, of course you don't, or you wouldn't be asking!' She took a sip of her coffee then added more sugar. 'He's set up a trust, put a whole load of his own money in, and the income from the golf club and leisure centre will help with the upkeep, pay the helpers' wages. It's for disadvantaged kids—holidays, weekends. It's a brilliant idea— There'll be indoor activities as well as outdoor, a small farm, organic-produce gardens, riding, boating, fishing— It will let inner-city kids know there's more to life than hanging round street corners and getting into trouble.'

Long after Linda had left Caroline stayed in a mild state of shock. What the housekeeper had told her didn't gel with the picture of Ben Dexter she had built up in her mind: an arrogant, self-serving deceiver—a picture reinforced by his behaviour last night; his announcement that he'd won round one, as if he'd brought her here to engage in a battle. An announcement she'd been too filled with shame and embarrassment to question.

Had she been totally wrong about him? Had she misjudged him?

She pushed herself to her feet, putting the enigma that was Ben Dexter out of her mind. She had a job to do and it was pointless to waste her mental energies on a man who had as good as declared himself to be her enemy.

Bracing herself, she climbed the staircase to the room that had been her father's. The cumbersome Victorian wardrobes were empty as was the solitary chest of drawers, cleared out by the grieving Dorothy Skeet. The only piece of any value, the Italian, carved giltwood tester bed, which the housekeeper had sometimes shared, brought a lump to her throat.

She made a note of its likely value in the pad she carried and made a swift exit. Why had her father never loved her? Why had he actively disliked her?

Making a mental note to see Dorothy before she headed back to London she forced the memories of her troubled childhood to the back of her mind and carried on. The rooms that had been unused when her father had been alive were now cheerful and bright, either furnished with twin beds and colourful, functional chests and hanging cupboards, or made into bathrooms, ready for the youngsters who would be spending time here.

Ben must have invested a considerable amount of his private fortune in this charitable enterprise. Because he remembered his own deprived childhood?

The state had supported his mother, but only barely. Janet Dexter had tried to supplement her benefit by growing and selling fresh fruit and vegetables but the villagers, suspicious of the hard-eyed, grim-faced woman and her wild son, had refused to buy. Someone, she remembered now, had once threatened to report her pathetic entrepreneurial efforts to social security.

Life must have been tough for both of them, and what had brought mother and son to the village in the first place was unknown. Close as they had been during that long-ago summer, he had never talked about his earlier life. There were always things he'd kept hidden, even then.

Admiration for what he had made of himself, for his altruism where similarly disadvantaged children were concerned, made her bite her lip. She didn't want to think well of him. She couldn't afford to; she could so easily fall right back under his mesmeric spell, she admitted honestly. Last night had shown her that much.

Needing to keep her mental image of him sullied she reminded herself of the child he had fathered and had callously abandoned. Her own father had told her that Maggie Pope was a slut, had warned her not to have anything to do with her, ever, because if she did she'd be locked in her room until it was time to go back to school. Yet during those last traumatic days he'd said, 'Ask Maggie Pope who fathered that brat of hers. Dexter. You don't believe me? Well, just go and ask her!'

Caroline shuddered, her body suddenly cold, as if she'd been immersed in icy water. It had been the worst day of her life and she didn't want to relive it, but couldn't stop the pictures that flashed into her mind.

The baby girl, around two months old at that time, had had silky black hair, just like Ben's, and Maggie had said sourly, 'Sure she's his. Only he don't want to know—that's his sort all over. Drop a girl as soon as the novelty's over, or someone tastier comes along—no sense of responsibility!'

Swallowing hard, Caroline forced her mind back to the job in hand. At the far end of the corridor, where the old Tudor wing joined the main part of the house, there had been a handsome mahogany linen press. But, like most of the other pieces of any value, it had gone. Irritation pricked her. Her professional appraisal was unnecessary. The few pieces of any value would be obvious to anyone. Ben Dexter had got her here under false pretences.

But why?

Automatically, her hand lifted to the latch on the oak-boarded door that led to the old wing. These rooms, over the kitchen regions, had been forbidden to her as a child. 'Full of spiders and creepy-crawlies, and the floorboards are rotten,' Dorothy Skeet had warned, and she'd been eight years old before she'd plucked up the courage to poke her nose in.

Now all was changed. Crumbling timbers had been replaced with silvery oak beams and sunlight streamed in through the windows, enriching the colours of the Persian rugs on the polished floor of what was clearly the sitting room of the suite Ben had reserved for his own use, the attractively furnished room dominated by the painting that had thrown them together again. *First Love.*

She caught her breath, her heart starting to thud. If Michael hadn't recognised the lost Lassoon masterpiece for what it was, or if Ben hadn't wanted to own it, then her life would have gone on smoothly, the old, painful yearnings would never have resurfaced so strongly because she and Ben would not have met again.

Her bones tightened rigidly as she stared up at what could have been her mirror image. She and Ben had spent a couple of blissfully happy, ecstatic months together and his betrayal had been cruel. But it had been twelve years ago, for pity's sake. It should have been written off to experience, forgotten.

But it hadn't.

'You approve?' His voice was silky-soft.

Caroline gave an involuntary jerk of her head, startled out of her tormenting thoughts. Then she turned reluctantly to face him, her violet eyes huge in the delicate pallor of her face.

He was looking particularly spectacular in a beautifully cut dark blue suit, crisp white shirt and sober tie. At the back of the house she hadn't heard his car draw up outside. If she had she would have taken evasive action. As it was she could only answer his question, 'It's your painting, it's up to you where you hang it. Though I hope you have some sort of security system.'

'There speaks the prosaic Caroline Harvey.' He was smiling, just slightly, but his eyes were cold, like splinters of polished jet. 'But let's take the larger view, shall we? Don't you agree that the portrait should be here, back at home, as it were?' Laughter was lurking in the curl of his voice now. It incensed her.

'Rubbish!' she said stoutly. He was playing games with her and she wasn't going to let him amuse himself at her expense. 'You're talking as if that's a portrait of me hanging on that wall—and you know damned well it isn't. Now, if you'll excuse me—'

'But it could be, couldn't it?' he inserted smoothly. 'You, as I remember you. After I'd read the article about its discovery, saw the photograph, I knew I had to have that painting and hang it here. As a reminder that things aren't always as they seem. The sitter looks like you, but she isn't. Just as you, when I knew you, weren't what I thought you were.'

'That's a case of the pot calling the kettle black if ever I heard one!' she said in sharp retaliation. This was a man with a serious grudge. Had he resented so badly that letter saying she never wanted to see him again? Was his ego still smarting over being dumped for once, after all this time?

This was getting far too deep for her. She was leaving. This very minute.

'Mr Dexter,' she said, schooling her voice to what she hoped would pass as icy coolness. 'There is no point in my being here any longer. My professional services weren't required in the first place. As far as I can see you've already disposed of most of the worthless furnishings and kept less than a handful of good pieces. I'll let you have Weinberg's evaluation of their worth in writing.'

'How kind.' One dark brow was elevated mockingly. He was blocking the doorway and to get out of here she'd have to brush right past him. Close to him. She couldn't face that. Just being in the same room with him made her feel weak all over.

Caroline swallowed convulsively and Ben drawled, 'You were right about your professional services not being needed. But I have other needs, Caro, and you are going to satisfy every last one of them. Only then will you be free to go.'

He gave her a slow, thoughtful look, 'I suggest we stop pussy-footing around and start right now.'

CHAPTER SIX

'NOW, why would I agree to do that?' Caroline queried, facing him with a poise she was miles away from feeling. Her heart was thumping wildly, her flesh quivering on her bones.

A long time ago they'd satisfied each other's needs completely—was that what he was suggesting? Had last night been a slow, cruelly teasing prelude to an inexorable seduction? The palms of her hands were slick now and drops of perspiration beaded her forehead, gathered in the cleft between her breasts as she was torn between jangling nervousness and helpless excitement.

'Because you owe me,' he retorted heavily, his narrowed eyes holding hers then dropping to rest on her mouth. 'You owe me for twelve, wasted years.'

Her brain told her to walk out of here, pack her bags and phone for a taxi. He couldn't hold her here by force. But her heart was beating in compelling opposition, telling her to stay.

That their long-ago tempestuous love affair had left an indelible mark on him too, given his love-'em-and-leave-'em attitude to women, was shattering. Perhaps it was mischievous fate that had brought them back together because it was finally time to close the circle and at last shut the past away where it belonged.

She couldn't walk away from this, this final confrontation, if that was what it was. 'Judging by your impressive achievements, the last twelve years can hardly be called a waste,' she managed to say, desperately striving to bring an air of factual normality into a conversation that was in danger of becoming unreal: Unreal to believe that she could have wounded his psyche as he, she now admitted helplessly, had so deeply wounded hers.

'That's not what I'm talking about, and I think you know it.' Two paces brought Ben to stand directly in front of her, his wide-shouldered stance overpowering her senses. Holding her huge violet eyes with the shadowed darkness of his he removed his suit jacket, slowly tossing it onto the nearest armchair, then loosened his tie.

Caroline's mouth went dry. She took a quick, ragged intake of breath. She could feel the heat of that intensely virile body just inches from her own, and the heat was melting her.

Instinctively, her tongue peeped out to moisten the aridity of her lips, lips that suddenly felt too full and lush. And his brooding eyes followed the involuntary, betraying movement and he said soberly, 'Ah, yes, I remember that nervous little gesture from moments before the first kiss we ever shared. And exactly how I helped—like this, remember, Caro?' His dark head dipped as his mouth met hers, no other part of their bodies touching, his tongue laving the quivering fullness of her lower lip, leaving the sensitised skin slick and supple, finding the parting, making an easy entry to the helplessly willing sweetness within.

Her blood sang, the electric brush of his lips and tongue was just as she remembered, the pleasure almost too much to bear. As much as she wanted to close the tiny distance between them, to wrap her arms around him, press her aching breasts and thighs against the hard maleness of him, she resisted. The slow, seductive melding of their mouths was exquisite torment enough.

And it should not be happening, the last dying vestige of common sense reminded her, acidly recalling his off-hand rejection of the night before.

But the voice died, drowned in the clamour of her raging pulse beats. His love-making had always been a drug, something she couldn't do without. Something her body had been silently crying for during these last barren, lonely years.

When he lifted his head after timeless, delirious moments his breathing was as ragged as her own, his fingers not quite steady as he reached to take the tortoiseshell clip from her hair, setting it free to fall in midnight-dark glossy abandon to her shoulders.

'It used to be much longer,' he murmured thickly. 'It used to cloak your breasts with silk, inviting me to kiss the rosy buds that hid behind it. You knew how to tantalise me, Caro. Do you remember?'

Remember? How could she ever forget? Memories of how wonderful and perfect they'd been together had always been buried deep in her mind, not taken out and examined—she'd learned more control than that—but there all the same, indelibly imprinted, denying her any sexual interest in any other man.

Had it been the same for him? The concept was difficult to take in, especially as her brain seemed to have stopped working.

Slowly, with explicit intent, he began to undo the tiny buttons of her shirt, his eyes focused on what he was doing, the backs of his fingers grazing her burning skin, making her incapable of any coherent response when he said darkly, 'Twelve years is a long time, Caro. Too damned long to be left in limbo.'

He slid the shirt from her shoulders and bent to briefly suckle her blatantly engorged nipples through the creamy lace of her bra and she whimpered softly with the tormenting pleasure of the short, insistent tugs of his mouth. She laid her hands against his chest, palms down, feeling the heat and vibrant strength of him, the heavy beats of his heart and knew she would soon be unable to stand without support because every last one of her bones had turned to water.

'Years of wanting what most men want, a wife, a family,' Ben asserted, his voice holding a trace of bitterness. His knuckles pressed against the softly feminine curve of her tummy as, having disposed of her belt and dealt with the zip he began to slide her trousers down over her hips. 'Of wanting a good, long-term relationship and not being able to deliver, of being unable to commit to any other woman because no other woman came close to what I remembered of you.'

Naked now, apart from insubstantial briefs and bra, she was open to his darkly anguished eyes, vulnerable, captivated by him as she always had been, but pricked to suspicion by the strong note of torment in his voice.

Treachery! her internal warning system whispered and she said, almost incoherently, 'You bought that painting—'

'As a reminder that things are not always what they seem, or what you want them to be,' he repeated. And then, as if he saw the beginnings of understanding, of resistance in her eyes, he laid a finger across her mouth, 'Don't speak. Just give yourself to the moment,' and enfolded her in his arms, his mouth finding the tender hollow just below her ear, his lips moving with slow eroticism as he murmured, 'You always liked this, and you still do, don't you? Admit it, Caro.'

As if the tiny moan that escaped her was admission enough he lifted her in his arms, holding her close as he carried her into the adjoining bedroom.

A hazy impression of a cool masculine atmosphere, the tiny-paned windows open to the warm spring air admitting the perfume of early-flowering honeysuckle, a carved oak bed. A huge bed.

Her unresisting body sank into the soft duvet as he laid her down and removed the last scraps of creamy lace. 'As perfect as ever.' His dark gaze caressed her nakedness. 'The years have been kind to you, Caro.'

The slight catch in his voice touched her heart with pain. Instinctively, she held out her arms to him, needing to hold him close, to banish whatever it was that was hurting him. But he straightened up, his beautiful mouth forming the command, 'Wait', and began to unbutton his shirt, removing it, and then those elegantly tailored trousers, tossing the expensive garments aside as if they were old dusters.

His lean, whippy young adult's body had matured spectacularly; His shoulders wide and strong, his chest deep and faintly dusted with dark hair. Yet there wasn't an ounce of spare flesh beneath the olive-toned skin that gleamed with health and vitality.

Caroline swallowed awkwardly around the sudden lump in her throat. Fully aroused, he was magnificent and the air throbbed with expectancy, with the inevitability of what was happening between them and, as he lowered himself beside her, laying his hand on the heated mound of her aching desire she searched his face for the lover he had been, longing to find him again, to hear the words of white-hot passion he had bewitched and had captivated her with, longing with an intensity that shook her slight frame and set her veins on fire.

But as his gently questing fingers found the slick core of her and just before his mouth took hers in a drugging kiss, he murmured raggedly, 'You want me, and I need this. I need, finally, to prove to myself that what you were to me is only in my mind. That you're no different from any other woman.'

She must have fallen asleep. The earth-shattering, multi-climaxes of their love-making, coupled with the near sleepless night had exhausted her. Caroline struggled to come properly awake beneath the light warmth of the duvet. Twilight filled the room and she was alone.

Of course she was alone. Tears stung the back of her eyes and tightened her throat. Ben had calculatedly used her, had got her out of his system. It was as simple and as devastating as that.

When he'd told her exactly how and why he was using her she'd been too far gone in the sexual delirium that only he could make happen to do the right thing: to slap his sinfully beautiful, arrogant face and walk away.

Tears coursed unheeded down her pale cheeks. They were both damned: he for so cold-bloodedly using her, she for allowing it to happen.

But his blood hadn't been cold, had it? Hot, white-hot passion had driven him and she—she had been incandescent.

Angrily, she swiped at her wet cheeks with the back of her hand and scrambled off the bed, snatching up her bra and briefs and scampering through to the sitting room to collect the rest of her discarded clothing. Throwing them on all anyhow, not because she was afraid Ben might walk in on her—he had got what he wanted and probably wouldn't want to see her any more than she wanted to have to face him—but because she had to get out of this house, the house that had never, in all of her life, held any happiness for her.

It was too late now to make the necessary arrangements to get back to London. Besides, she felt emotionally wrung out, in no fit state.

Tomorrow she would feel better. Later tonight she would pack and first thing in the morning she would phone for a taxi to take her into Shrewsbury, get the inter-city back to London, get her life back on track again.

Ben wouldn't complain to her boss, she decided cynically. She'd satisfied those needs he'd talked about and he'd be more than happy to see her go.

Outside the air was cooler than she'd expected but she wasn't going back in to fetch a jacket, not when it meant risking running into Ben. Hell would freeze over before she could meet his eyes without cringing with shame.

Unthinking, her mind pre-programmed, Caroline skirted the property, crossed the walled kitchen gardens and let herself out onto the green lane beyond the wooden door in the far wall. The grass was soft beneath her feet and soon she was under the dim canopy of the trees that bordered the stream.

The sound of the water as it chattered over its stony bed soothed her a little. The rustle of ferns as she brushed through them and the cry of a distant owl eased some of the tension from her shoulders.

She rubbed some warmth into her arms, the thin

silk of her shirt offering little protection from the cool evening air, and stepped into a grassy clearing. The mist from the water made softly moving grey patterns against the dark background of the trees.

She saw him then and stopped breathing. Too late she realised where she'd come, instinctively making her way, as she had so often done in the past, to the secret place. The secluded, magical place where their love had been consummated, where dreams had been born and nourished. Dreams that had turned into a nightmare of betrayal and deceit.

How could she have been so thoughtless? And, more to the point, why was he here?

Ben had his back to her, standing on the bank of the stream, seemingly intent on the dark waters as they swirled around the partly submerged rocks. Caroline turned swiftly to retrace her steps but he must have heard her.

He called her name.

The sound of his voice sent shock waves through her. Her feet felt as if they were rooted to the ground. She could hear his approach and still couldn't move.

'Don't go.' He sounded weary, as if something had happened to drain away his life force. 'I have to talk to you.'

Caroline didn't want to hear what he had to say, whatever it was. He diminished her utterly, made her so ashamed of herself.

Clinging onto what little dignity that remained, she said dully, 'I'm going back. It's getting very dark and I'm cold.'

'Then, I'll walk with you,' he said firmly, adding, 'Wait!' as she took a blind step back into the woodland. The touch of his hand as he laid it on her shoulder was sheer torture, the warmth and strength of it sending sparks through her that were part pleasure, part agonising pain.

He turned her round, his eyes searching her face and even in the fading light she could see the faint, almost reluctant, smile that curved his mouth. 'Your shirt's buttoned up all wrongly and your hair's gone mad—you look exactly like the wild thing I used to know. Here—' Releasing her briefly, he slipped out of the soft leather jacket he wore over a body-hugging dark T-shirt and draped it over her shoulders.

The masculine warmth of him, stored in the supple leather, almost defeated her, but not nearly as much as the sudden shocking and heart-stopping realisation that, whatever he had been in the past, whatever he was now, she still loved him.

Her stomach churned sickeningly. But he didn't love her. He never had, despite his youthful protestations. The sex had been brilliant, that was all.

Today he'd admitted that his need to form a committed relationship with any other woman had been stifled by the memory of their tempestuous, perfect love-making.

She could understand that, sympathise. Memories could be dangerous, distorting things. So he'd made love to her, had used her to satisfy himself that she was just an ordinary woman, no different from any other.

She had set him free, free to do what he'd said he wanted—commit himself to one special woman, marry, raise children. Did that explain his gentler mood, the care he was taking on her behalf as he guided her through the growing darkness? Resignedly, she supposed it did.

Emerging from the trees she caught her foot on a root and would have fallen had the guiding arm around her waist not tightened, pulling her against his body.

She heard the rough tug of his breath, felt the heavy beats of his heart beneath the palms of her hands that had automatically splayed out, seeking support. Felt the immediate masculine stir of his body and pulled away. Easy to go with the flow, take what there was to take of him in the short time they had left together. But dangerous for her future peace of mind. What had happened this afternoon must not happen again.

Away from the trees the going was easier, the light from billions of stars making his guiding, protective arm redundant. She mourned the loss though she knew she shouldn't and the silence he kept—in spite of his saying that he needed to talk to her—was like an intolerable ache.

She would be leaving early in the morning she reminded herself so perhaps this was their final goodbye. Recriminations for the heartless way he'd used her—both in the past and since their paths had crossed again—would achieve nothing.

No one was all bad and, as they reached the house, she knew she had to tell him how much she admired what was good in him.

Caroline waited while he closed the door behind them and flicked on the lights, the aching sadness inside her robbing her voice of all vitality as she said, 'Linda told me what you're doing with this house—helping children from deprived backgrounds. I think it's wonderful—'

'You do?' His eyes, the set of his mouth was dismissive. Plainly he wasn't interested in compliments, not if they came from her. 'Ironic, isn't it? I saved your revered family home from falling into complete disrepair, only to plan to fill it with young tearaways from run-down estates. Your father would turn in his grave if he knew that his precious daughter would have to face such a situation.' One brow rose mockingly. 'The villagers used to call you Princess Caroline, did you know that? Shut away in your ivory tower, too good to mix with the likes of them.'

This barely veiled antagonism was enough to break her heart, especially as she recognised the truth that she'd so carefully hidden from herself for such a long time. She could never love another man as she loved this one: warts and all.

Misery, coupled with anger at the hand fate had dealt her, made her voice thick and throaty as she countered, 'Of course I knew! It was unfair and it hurt! And as far as my father was concerned I would never be coming back here. He finally disowned me and threw me out when I refused to fall in with his plans and get engaged to Jeremy.'

She saw his quick frown, heard the sharp intake of his breath as he asked, 'Is that true? Your father said the engagement was planned for your eighteenth birthday—only a few weeks away, that the marriage would take place early the following spring.'

'Really!'

She couldn't entirely blame her father. He had only been saying what he'd believed to be the truth, that he could, as usual, coerce her into doing exactly what he told her to do. But she could blame Dexter for taking her father's statement at face value and deciding that she'd been using him, having a sneaky affair on the side, enjoying—what had he called it?—rough trade!

'And when did that conversation take place?' she queried bitterly, 'When he offered you money to make yourself scarce?'

'Yes.'

The simple, unrepentant affirmative rocked her. Stupidly, she'd been hoping that he'd categorically deny ever having taken that pay-off, that his betrayal hadn't been as thorough and as cruel as she'd believed, that her father had lied.

Her shoulders slumping, she removed his jacket and dropped it on the floor. She felt so tired and empty now it was an effort to stand upright. Bed. Sleep. That was what she needed. Tomorrow the traumatic happenings of this day would be behind her and she could go on.

She took a faltering step towards the staircase and heard him say gently, 'What happened this afternoon was a shock for me, too, Caro. I guess I'm only just coming out of it. No, don't go—' She took another jerky step towards the escape route of the stairs. 'Hear me out, please. I want you to forget we have a history. I want you to marry me.'

CHAPTER SEVEN

CAROLINE turned quickly. Too quickly. Her head swam dizzily. She would have fallen if Ben hadn't slipped an arm around her and held her, pulling her against the broad, hard wall of his chest.

His blunt, out-of-the-blue proposal was the very last thing she'd expected. Her acceptance, should she be crazy enough to give it, would throw up implications she didn't think she'd be able to handle.

Marrying Ben Dexter had once been her most precious dream but now, after all that had happened and the passage of so many years, it was totally out of the question. Her shoulders shook with the onset of hysteria and her sudden, unstoppable and totally humiliating tears soaked the front of his T-shirt.

'Don't cry,' he said soothingly. 'Please don't. I shouldn't have landed that on you so suddenly.' Strong hands on her slender shoulders held her slightly away, his fingers brushing away the wetness from her cheeks, his dark eyes sweeping over her troubled features. 'I don't expect an answer right now, Caro. You'll need time to think about it. I've been mulling it over ever since you fell asleep in my arms, so I've had a head start.'

He dropped a light kiss on her quivering mouth, his eyes smiling now, bringing all his forceful charisma into play as he slipped an arm back around her waist and insisted wryly, 'We'll both feel less disorientated if we eat. I'll throw something on the stove while you choose the wine.'

Resisting the strong desire to disintegrate into further hysterics Caroline dragged air through her pinched nostrils and blurted, 'I can't marry you, you know I can't—it was a crazy thing to ask!'

She felt utterly confused and deeply upset and his lazy 'Why?' did nothing to help. Breathing unevenly, she pulled away from him. Ever since she'd returned to Langley Hayes she'd lost her grip on reality. Somehow or other she had to regain it.

'Because,' she said more steadily, determined now to gather her defences against the man her treacherous body and stupid heart craved so desperately, 'what you feel for me is simply lust—not to mention contempt. Marriage couldn't possibly work out.'

'Contempt; yes, there was that,' he admitted softly after a pause no longer than a heartbeat. 'For a long time now I've believed you were planning to marry the Curtis fortune while having a furtive affair with me. That sort of conviction is difficult to shake off. You see, way back then, I wanted to ask you if it was true, about Curtis, but when I got back I found that letter telling me it was all over between us, that you never wanted to set eyes on me again. As far as I was concerned it confirmed everything your father had told me.'

He walked into her line of vision, his hands bunched into his trouser pockets, his dark eyes moody. 'I had to go that day; there was no choice. With hindsight I know I should have told you of my plans, explained why I used to disappear for days, but I wasn't sure things would work out.' His mouth compressed wryly. 'I guess I was misguided but I wanted to present you—everyone—with a tangible success, not a pipedream.

'For over a year Jim Mays—an old friend from up north—and I had been trying to set up in the software business. We met up now and then to develop ideas. Then, that day, right after my disastrous meeting with your father, Jim phoned me, told me to drop everything and get down to London because he'd found a potential backer who would only be available for a few hours that day. But all the while we were pitching I was desperate to get back and get the truth from you.

'But the moment I did get back Mother gave me your letter—giving me the brush-off in no uncertain terms, and from then on I thought you were every kind of bitch. Now I prefer to believe your version of events, that your father threw you out because you refused to marry Curtis. As for your Dear John, looking back I guess we can put that down to cold feet. You were very young at the time. So forget the contempt side of it, Caro, it no longer exists.'

He shrugged slightly, his mouth indented. 'And, as for lust, what's wrong with that? It's nature's way of ensuring the survival of the species, so don't knock it. OK, I admit to the crass sin of getting you here under false pretences. I wanted to prove to myself that you were nothing special and all I did was prove that you were very special indeed. We're dynamite together; no other woman comes near you as far as I'm concerned. You're a singing in my blood, a desperate hunger—this afternoon proved that much.' His voice thickened. 'And I think—no, I know, you felt it too. It's not finished Caro; it's lasted twelve long years; it's an undying fever.'

His words bewildered, delighted and terrified her. She could so easily ignore common sense and give in to the craving to marry the man she loved, to take what she could of him for the time it lasted.

She put her fingers to her temples in the age-old gesture of despair. The time it lasted would be short. How could it be otherwise when he was motivated only by lust and long memory of an incomparable, magical summer, and she by a love that was tainted with mistrust?

True, he had come back to find the truth from all that time ago. But that underlined his deceit. He had come back despite having taken a wad of her father's cash in return for the promise to stay away.

Unconsciously, she shook her head. 'Sex isn't everything, no matter how brilliant it is. So, OK—' she gave him a tired smile '—I admit that what we once had made such an impression that, like you, apparently, it's hard to find a partner that measures up. But the bottom line is, Ben, you deceived and cheated on us all—Father, Maggie Pope, me. People don't change, not basically. I would always be waiting for it to happen again.'

And when that happened she would be destroyed. Utterly, totally and completely.

The hall clock struck the hour, nine sonorous beats, and Ben said darkly, 'What the hell are you talking about?' Then he swore softly, almost inaudibly as the doorbell chimed. 'Wait.' He flung the word at her tersely. 'I'll get rid of whoever it is and then you can tell me what you meant.'

She registered the irritated set of his wide shoulders, the impatience of his long-legged stride as he crossed the hall, and she shivered.

He was everything she'd ever wanted and the white heat of their young passion had ruined her emotional life for years as, so it would seem, it had ruined his. That being the case, she could understand and even forgive his cold-blooded attempt to get her out of his system.

But that hadn't happened, had it? Their love-making this afternoon had been better than ever, spiced with a deeper, sweeter poignancy. So, to use that hoary phrase 'marry or burn' he had decided to propose.

And she was burning now, flames of forbidden excitement leaping inside her because despite knowing it would be emotional suicide she wanted to accept his proposal so badly it was like an invisible hoist, drawing her inexorably to him.

Perhaps, after he'd sent the caller away, they could sort things out.

If he should tell her he deeply regretted his behaviour towards Maggie and now gave her and the daughter he'd turned his back on all those years ago financial and moral support…

If he told her he had had every intention of returning the money her father had given him, admitting that he wasn't prepared, after all, to stay away…

But he was holding the door wide, his inborn politeness to the fore as he said, 'Of course you're not being a nuisance. She's right here. Please do come in.'

Dorothy Skeet emerged slowly into the lighted hall. The years had solidified her plumpness into corpulence and her once blondish fluffy hair had turned to dull pepper and salt. She said uncertainly, 'I heard you were here, Miss Caroline, but I didn't know for how long. It's a bit late, I know, but I didn't want to miss you.'

Caroline's heart skipped a beat and, awkwardly at first and then more surely, she crossed the floor to hug the older woman. Her throat felt clogged with the tears that now seemed perilously and uncharacteristically near the surface. The only kindness—albeit casual—she'd known in this house had come from this lady.

'Why don't we all go through?' Ben said into the ensuing, emotionally charged silence. 'I was about to make supper, why don't you join us, Dorothy?'

'Oh, I couldn't!—I mean, I've already had my tea,' she said, flustered, her round face turning pink. 'I didn't want to intrude, I only came to hand over your dad's things.' She fumbled at the catch on her capacious handbag, suspiciously over-bright eyes now clinging to Caroline's.

The older woman was clearly ill at ease and Caroline didn't know what to say to make her feel more comfortable. It was Ben who came to the rescue, his smile as irresistible as ever as he suggested, 'Then, come and sit with us while we eat. Enjoy a glass of wine—or coffee if you prefer, and spill all the village gossip. I know Caro wants to catch up with everything that's been going on these last few years.'

That was news to her, but the fabrication was worth it, Caroline thought as Dorothy's eyes lit up at the prospect and she became instantly more relaxed.

Her father's former housekeeper had an incorrigible and unrepentant appetite for gossip and she wondered if the older woman had somehow found out about her and Ben's secret affair, or had heard gossip in the village and had passed it on to her father. If so it would explain why she'd initially appeared so uncomfortable when encountering the two of them together.

Trailing behind Ben and Dorothy as they headed for the kitchen, Caroline dismissed the thought. It was no longer important. Let the past stay in the past.

Even if her father had remained ignorant of what had been going on and she and Ben had married quietly as soon as she was eighteen, as she'd suggested on more than one occasion, the result would have been the same: their relationship would have broken up in pain and disillusionment when the inevitable happened and she learned of his abandoned little daughter.

The sobering knowledge was something she was going to have to keep in the forefront of her mind. Something to stiffen her resolve to turn that astonishing proposal of marriage down flat and not give in to the weakness of her love for the deceiving monster that kept creeping up on her whenever she let her mental guard down.

How could she, even in a weak moment, contemplate marriage with a man whose past record made her cringe, whose only real interest in her was the slaking of a lust that hadn't died, despite all their years apart?

But despite her angst-ridden thoughts it was hard to stay in a sombre mood whilst Dorothy Skeet, sipping at the mug of hot cocoa which was her preferred tipple at this time of night, regaled them with the latest village gossip, sometimes hilarious and often downright slanderous, while Caroline herself, finding an appetite that surprised her, tucked into the succulent grilled gammon and tomatoes Ben had rustled up.

'Don't believe half of it.' Ben grinned as he refilled both their wine glasses and motioned Dorothy to stay where she was when she made to clear the table. 'Every time a story's told it gathers a whole new and highly coloured dimension!'

'Too true!' Caroline smiled right back at him over the rim of her glass. The relaxed atmosphere, the simple food and superb wine, the laughter, Ben's comical mock-horror as he threw up his hands and rolled his eyes at some of Dorothy's more wicked comments, had taken the stress out of the situation.

So when the older woman took a tissue-wrapped bundle from her handbag and handed it to her Caroline was able to view her father's few personal effects without the familiar clutch of misery in the region of her heart.

The silver fob-watch he had always worn tucked into his waistcoat pocket complete with chain and onyx seal, the gold signet ring that had come down from his father and was now thin with age, two fountain pens—not much to show for sixty-odd years of living.

But her sense of loss was deep as she folded the tissue over the pathetic mementos. However she did her best not to let it show as she placed the package back into Dorothy's hands.

'I know my father would have liked you to keep these,' she said gently.

Dorothy had been Reginald Harvey's bed companion for many years. On her part it had been love, on his a blunt and probably infrequently expressed affection. Seeing the doubt in the other woman's eyes, Caroline insisted. 'He was fond of you, he was closer to you than anyone. He—' her voice faltered, thickened, but she forced the words out '—he actively disliked me. I know he would rather you had these keepsakes.'

She heard the intake of Ben's breath followed by

a beat of a silence so thick she could almost taste it. Strangely, although she knew it should be otherwise, his presence gave her the strength to add, 'In return, you could tell me why—why he never seemed able to stand the sight of me. You must have gathered some clues over the years. And maybe—' she tugged in a deep breath, feeling Ben's dark eyes on her, feeling his unspoken compassion '—maybe if I knew why, I could forgive him.'

'Yes,' the older woman concurred, her eyes darkening with sympathy even as her fingers tightened around the keepsakes. 'He was close-lipped where his feelings were concerned but he adored your mother—anyone who saw them together knew that—he worshipped the ground she walked on. Jane Bayliss—you'll remember her, she married old Hume the butcher—worked here at the time, cleaning and such; she said she was sure he had mixed feelings when your mum got pregnant with you. He didn't want anyone, even his own child, to have any of her attention. He wanted it all for himself.'

Caroline's brow furrowed. Had her father really loved that obsessively? Then she remembered the letters she'd found in the attic and knew that he had. He'd loved her mother as single-mindedly and deeply as he'd disliked his only child.

Her eyes misting, she said quietly, her voice barely audible, 'And she died when I was very small.' That much she did know. Her father had never talked to her about her mother, apart from angrily stating that bald fact when she'd pressed him for details. Truth to tell, he'd rarely spoken to her at all, except to issue curt instructions and even curter reprimands.

'She died an hour after you were born,' Dorothy supplied, shaking her head. 'It was the talk of the area at the time, a terrible tragedy. You came three weeks early, at the beginning of November.

'There'd been a surprise heavy snowstorm overnight. Appalling drifts—your dad couldn't get your mum out and no one could get through. You came quickly and your mum haemorrhaged badly, and by the time the emergency helicopter and paramedics arrived it was already too late—all this came out at the inquest.

'When I got the job as housekeeper I saw how your dad treated you and it's my guess he bitterly resented the fact that you had lived and his wife had died.' She gave a heavy sigh. 'You grew up to be the living image of her, but you weren't her.'

'So he couldn't bear to have me around,' Caroline said huskily. 'He blamed me.'

'I thought the world of him. Well, you know that, but I wasn't afraid to let him know he was treating you wrong—even if he did tell me to mind my own damn business,' Dorothy conceded. 'It wasn't your fault, you didn't ask to be born. I did tell him that, more than once. And later, he started to soften up a bit. But by then it was too late. You'd grown prickly and defiant. A terrible shame, really.' She got slowly to her feet. 'I really should go now, but I'm glad we talked.'

'I'll drive you.'

Even as Ben made the offer Caroline was conscious of his smouldering gaze; it burned her where it touched. When they'd been together all those years ago he had known she and her father didn't get along but had been unaware of how deep the rift was. She hadn't wanted to talk about her unhappy home life, only about the future they'd planned together.

'No need,' Dorothy stated. 'I came in my old rattle-trap.'

'Then, I'll see you out.'

Caroline smothered a groan. Right now she didn't want Ben's sympathy or his company. She needed time to herself to come to terms with the mess she and her father had made of their relationship, to mourn that final interview when she had screamed at him, vowing she'd rather die than do what he wanted and marry Jeremy, telling him she didn't care if he carried out his threat to throw her out because she never wanted anything more to do with him.

Seventeen going on eighteen, her heart broken and bleeding because of her lover's betrayal, she'd been in no mood for conciliatory words, to soberly tell him that she could never marry the Curtis wealth because she didn't, and never would, love Jeremy Curtis. In too much pain herself to consider her father's possible hurt when she'd declared that she hated him and always had.

It was too late now to retract the bitter words, to tell him she forgave him for not having been able to love her as a father should have because, at last, she understood the reason for his resentment of her.

Her shoulders shook as she buried her head in her hands, her sobs overwhelming her. Only when she felt the light touch of Ben's hand on the top of her head did she make a determined but not too successful effort to pull herself together.

'Don't,' he said softly as he cupped her elbows and pulled her to her feet, his arms holding her close. 'Tonight you learned something you hadn't known before and naturally enough it's upset you. But your father treated you abominably, Caro. His memory doesn't deserve this amount of grief.'

He framed her tear-stained face with long-fingered hands, his thumbs stroking back tendrils of raven-dark hair. 'He was a man obsessed by the memory of his one great love and I can understand that, but not his treatment of an innocent child. If the two of you were estranged for the last years of his life it wasn't your fault.'

Caroline shook her head mutely, her breath shaking in her lungs, her fingers clutching his shoulders convulsively, as if she could take strength from the warm solidity of muscle and bone. The compassion and caring in his beautiful eyes, in the tender set of that sensual mouth, made her tremble, taking her back through the years to the place she had been when he'd not only been her first and devastatingly exciting lover but her very best friend, a rock she could have clung to in any storm.

Her soft lips parting, she managed a shaky, 'No.' Then, more steadily, she confessed sadly, 'When I was little I wanted him to love me more than anything in the world. But I knew he didn't. Sometimes I saw him looking at me as if he hated me. I thought it was my fault, that there was something horrible about me.'

She shook her head, silencing him when he gave a growl of repudiation deep in his throat. 'Dorothy was right on two counts. At one time he did try to build bridges, to take an interest when I was home for school holidays, asking about the friends I'd made, what books I was reading.'

She scooped in a shaky breath. 'But it was too late. I was a defiant fifteen by then, used to being pushed away, ignored. I shrugged away any overture he tried to make, stuck my nose in the air and walked away, letting him know I didn't need him, didn't need anyone.' She gave a shaky sigh. 'That was the end of any hope of any harmony in our spiky relationship. I bitterly regret it now.'

His body tensed against hers and there was the shadow of a catch in his voice as he told her, 'That reaction would have been entirely natural, given the circumstances. You truly don't have to regret it. The only thing you should regret is the fact that his treatment of you made you wary of—or incapable of—committing to a permanent relationship. I understand that.'

He didn't understand at all, she thought wearily. She would have committed the rest of her life to Ben if things hadn't gone so badly wrong, if he hadn't deceived her. But right now she was too drained to put him straight on that score, and her head fell forward, resting against the solid expanse of his chest.

All she wanted was the oblivion of sleep, to rid her tired brain of aching regrets, of the confusion of her heart and body wanting and needing this one man with something approaching ferocity and her brain telling her in no uncertain terms that he wasn't to be trusted.

So when he murmured, 'You're emotionally drained, sweetheart. We'll talk again in the morning. Right now you need sleep,' she could only nod in thankful agreement and push away the admonitory voice in her brain that told her to object when he scooped her into his arms and carried her up to his room.

CHAPTER EIGHT

HIS bedroom. His bed. The covers still rumpled from this afternoon's wild love-making. Something electric quivered all the way through her.

Why had he brought her here instead of taking her to her own room? Silly question. He aimed to take advantage of her while she was stricken...

A low, self-denigrating moan escaped her as he slid her down the length of his body and set her on her feet. Who was she trying to fool? There was a fatal weakness in her where he was concerned, a deep craving that banished sanity and pride. And if he stayed this close to her one moment longer it would be she who would be taking advantage of him!

Wanton heat was already pooling between her thighs and something caught at the back of her throat as she raised the sultry heaviness of her lashes and let her glazed eyes roam the savagely handsome planes of his face, meeting the slightly frowning, brooding intensity of those gypsy dark eyes.

She shuddered convulsively as a wave of fierce longing flooded right through her. She needed to feel that sensually carved mouth on hers again, to take the thrusting masculine pride of his body into hers again—a need so desperate it ravaged her chaotic senses...

Her bones shaking, she reached out to him, but…

'You're out on your feet, sweetheart,' Ben remarked softly, placing his hands lightly on her shoulders, holding her upright as she swayed involuntarily towards him. 'Skip the shower tonight. You need sleep.'

The caring in his voice brought fresh tears to her eyes, mortifying her. She who never cried had shed enough to float a battleship over the past few hours.

Nothing to do with the trauma of at last learning just why her father had so bitterly resented her existence, nor the painful memories of that final interview—just Ben, his compassion. His caring for her well-being during their long-ago love affair had been one of the things that had made her love him so.

Yet that didn't gel with the way he'd washed his hands of any responsibility towards Maggie Pope and his baby daughter…

She muffled a sob as he began to undress her, peeling away her blouse then undoing the waistband of her linen trousers, the backs of his fingers grazing the soft, sensitised skin of her tummy.

Caroline gasped, her stomach muscles tightening as he slid the fabric down her hips. Did he know what he was doing—the effect he was having on her? How every nerve in her body leapt? How her heart was thundering wildly sending fire to every part of her in a raging torrent of need? How her breasts were swelling, the rosy peaks hard, aching for his mouth?

Risking a glance from under her lashes she saw that he didn't show even a casual interest in the twin globes he released as he unclipped her bra, merely dropping the filmy garment to the floor before turning his attention to her briefs with a smooth efficiency that made her burn with frustration.

Was he totally unaware of how wildly aroused she was, of how much she needed him? Did he think he was being considerate, leaving her in this state?

She thought she heard the sharp tug of his breath as she held onto him for balance while she shakily stepped out of the briefs he'd slid down the length of her legs, her engorged breasts brushing against him. And then she was sure she had to have imagined it when he laid almost clinical hands on her shoulders, turning her round then briskly plumping up the pillows, holding back the lightweight duvet, telling her levelly, 'In you get. I don't think you should be alone to brood tonight. So I'll be right beside you if you feel the need to talk, for someone to hold you. Just hold you, OK, Caro?'

A catch in her throat, she stumbled into the bed, felt the duvet settle upon her, heard him move away, heard the gush of the shower in the *en suite*, turned her face into the pillow and bit it. Hard.

It seemed hours before he joined her, the raging torment of wanting him so much it hurt making the sleep she needed impossible to come by.

He hadn't said a word when he'd finally exited the *en suite*. He'd simply walked across the room, switching off the light, closing the door to his private suite of rooms quietly behind him, leaving her alone in this room for what must have been ages.

Now Caroline heard the rustle of his clothing as he undressed in the darkness, felt the mattress dip as he slid in beside her, taking care not to disturb her.

Disturb her? She was disturbed enough to be in a white-hot sexual frenzy!

He settled down, his back to her, an aching void away in the huge bed. And she commanded thickly because she couldn't help it, because she was driven, 'Hold me, Ben. Please, hold me!'

She sensed him stiffen, the darkness around them tensing for one brief second before he turned and gathered her to him, folding his arms around her, tucking her head into the angle of his shoulder, his warm breath fanning her cheek as he murmured gently, 'I'm here, sweetheart. You'd like to talk?'

He too was naked. Her skin ignited against his, her blood exploding in her veins. Talk? They had to, of course they did. About Maggie, his child, the money he'd taken from her father. But not now.

Now she wanted him. Just him. The utter perfection of their physical mating, the bad things forgotten, just for now. Tomorrow would be soon enough for this fantasy of love to end, to tell him that she could never marry a man she couldn't trust.

'No!' she uttered hoarsely. 'Make love to me. I need you.' And she pressed her tingling breasts against the hard wall of his chest, wrapping her legs around his, drawing one of his thighs between hers, melting with delirium as she felt his instant, leaping response against the frantically quivering flesh of her abdomen. 'Now, Ben! Now!'

She heard him take a sudden breath and knew the control he'd been keeping had been fractured when he turned her on her back and straddled her. Then, with tormenting slowness he ran his hands down the length of her writhing body until he found the warm, secret dampness at the juncture of her thighs.

Caroline moaned aloud, his skilful fingers driving her to the point of no return and when his mouth replaced them she arched and bucked and cried his name as waves of ecstasy convulsed her, over and over, until she reached out and caught his head between her hands and kissed him, her breath sobbing raggedly in her lungs.

His own breathing was raw as he pulled her down with him and kicked away the duvet. Linking his fingers with hers he said with sultry confidence, 'That was for you. Now we do it my way, sweetheart. Slowly, very, very slowly…'

When Caroline woke she half expected to feel ashamed of her behaviour, but all she felt was a glorious wave of happiness and a sweet, drenching contentment.

She stirred and stretched lazily, voluptuously, and Ben's deep, honeyed voice said, 'Just like a lithe little cat.'

Lifting her lashes her soft amethyst eyes located him. Standing above her, clad in a short terry robe, his hair damp from the shower, he looked utterly gorgeous, the harsh, proud planes of his face curiously softened, his mouth a sultry, kissable curve.

Her heart wrenching over she hoisted herself back against the pillows as he put the two mugs of coffee he'd been carrying down on the bedside table then perched on the edge of the bed beside her.

'Now, there's a sight a man would gladly kill for,' he remarked silkily, his black eyes roaming her nakedness with languorous attention to every detail. 'Perfection against his pillows.'

His smile was so sexy it took her breath away, and she couldn't breathe at all when he dipped his dark head and lapped each tingling, pouting nipple then took her parted lips with an intimacy that blew her mind.

Her hands flew to his head, fingers tangling with the thick dark strands, as his tongue mimicked the staggering activities of the night, her body leaping with immediate, feverish response. But he drew away, his hands capturing hers, his eyes glinting wickedly beneath the lowered fan of his thick, spiky lashes.

'I've a proposition to put to you.'

Caroline dragged in a much needed breath as her heart twisted sharply. A proposition, not a proposal, thank the lord. She did not, most definitely not, want to have to think about his proposal of the evening before.

She didn't want to think of anything at all. The focus of her world, just for these few precious moments, was this man, the love for him that had burgeoned into strong, new life.

'We make today a holiday. We don't talk or think about anything but the two of us, the way we are now. The past, the future, won't get a mention.'

She saw a brief flicker of uncertainty in his eyes and gave him a glorious smile, assuring him throatily, 'That's absolutely fine by me!'

Couldn't be finer, in fact. Another magical twenty-four hours when reality didn't get a look in, when nothing bad marred the magic of letting herself drift with the flow of loving him.

'Then—' the wicked confidence was back in his eyes now, in the smile that curved the beautifully sculpted mouth as he reached over and put one of the delicate china mugs in her hand '—coffee first, followed by a shower—and it will be my pleasure to help you—and we'll take it from there.'

The shower took longer than any shower she'd ever taken before, the touch of his long fingers on every part of her soap-slicked body a new and decidedly erotic experience, just begging her to do the same to him, to share with him the intense pleasure she was feeling. And when he eased her back against the marble tiled wall, parted her trembling thighs and thrust possessively into her waiting body she knew that heaven couldn't offer a sweeter experience than this.

'I can't get enough of you.' His voice was still hoarse long after their mingled cries of rapture had been swallowed by the hiss of the water. 'It was always like this for us, remember?'

'Don't.' She placed her hand over his mouth to silence him. The writhing tendrils of steam made his features blurred, out of focus. 'We don't mention the past. We are simply what we are,' she reminded him, refusing to remember those long-gone good times because then she might have to remember the bad.

'And we are spectacular.' He grinned, conceding her point, reaching up to turn off the shower head.

And that she had to agree with, Caroline thought as he helped her out of the stall and wrapped her in a fluffy towel that smelt of sunshine and flowers. Cuddling into the folds she watched him, with dreamy eyes towel himself dry, drinking in the pagan splendour of his male physique, making one more memory to add to all the others.

As if he'd seen the sudden wistfulness behind her eyes, he reached out to cup the side of her face with one gentle hand. 'Mop yourself up and dress, sweetheart. I won't offer to do it for you because we wouldn't get breakfast before supper time if I did. Will toast and tea be enough, or shall I boil eggs?'

'Just toast,' she said croaking around the sudden lump in her throat. Was it still the lingering remnant of steam or had her eyes misted with tears? She certainly felt like weeping all over again. Today was meant to be a stolen slice of paradise, wasn't it? No room for looking back, or forward, no room for regrets, for tears.

She moved away, plucked a fresh towel from one

of the heated rails and wrapped it around her dripping hair, rubbing vigorously. When she emphasised, 'Tea and toast will be fine,' she sounded nicely cheerful.

Apparently satisfied, he walked through to the bedroom and she gave him ten minutes before she made her way to the room she'd been using. Passing the place where the mahogany linen press had once stood she had a sharp pang of conscience.

She really ought to get in touch with base, tell them she'd be returning in the morning. In view of the small amount of actual work she'd had to do here they'd wonder why it had taken her this long.

But she pushed the thought to the back of her mind. She'd phone first thing in the morning, before she set out. Today was hers. And Ben's. One more day out of a lifetime wasn't too much to ask, was it?

Tossing the things she'd worn the day before into her empty suitcase she slipped into clean silk undies and pondered what to wear as she stroked the brush through her damp hair. She didn't know what Ben's plans were but there was no one else in the house. The builders had removed the scaffolding yesterday morning, and the men currently at work making the golf course were on the opposite side of the estate.

Just the two of them, and whatever she put on wouldn't stay on for very long, she was sure of that. Her stomach wriggled at the thought, excited anticipation already building up inside her again. Just like the old times…

She brutally strangled the thought and picked up the faded, much washed jeans Linda had lent her.

They were indeed too wide and too short in the leg but she took the narrow leather belt from her own linen trousers and anchored the denim waist to her own much narrower one. Teamed with one of her own blouses, pale blue crêpe with short sleeves and a smooth V neckline, her bare feet pushed into her loafers, her hair a wild cloud falling to her shoulders, she looked nothing at all like the aloof, elegantly packaged career woman who had arrived here only a few short days ago.

The sudden rush of relief as she gazed at her haphazardly attired and comfortably unsophisticated reflection made her grin. She felt and looked more relaxed than she had done for years. Eschewing her usual, perfect make-up, she left the room, her feet on wings as she sped down to the kitchen.

Ben had gone ahead and boiled eggs anyway and the aroma of fresh coffee and warm toast made Caroline's mouth water. They were using the butcher's-block table beneath one of the sun-warmed windows and he'd produced honey and orange juice too.

'I can't remember ever eating such a huge breakfast,' she confessed, as she accepted a second cup of coffee after they'd stacked the used crockery in the dishwasher, wondering if she should loosen the narrow leather belt by a couple of notches.

'Then, maybe we should walk it off,' Ben suggested, smiling, as she drained her cup.

'Good idea.'

A beam of spring sunlight gleamed in his hair, touched the side of his forcefully handsome face and her heart swelled inside her breast. He was so gorgeous it sometimes hurt to look at him, and her body melted, just melted when he came to stand behind her, slipping his hands around her waist then slowly lifting them to cup her breasts.

He leant his face against the side of hers, his lips warm on her pinkening skin and she felt her breasts harden and fill the palms of his hands.

'Then, we'll head for the woods,' he murmured, adding silkily as his thumbs stroked her pouting nipples, 'Unless you have another form of exercise in mind?'

'Walk,' she said chokily, moving away. 'To begin with,' she added, but her smile was thin. They had always met in the woods, relishing the dark secrecy, their own precious privacy. The reminder put a heavy slab of sorrow in her heart.

She didn't want reminders, not today. Today was all they had left, and she would only be able to make it a happy memory if she didn't remember the past. So she wouldn't remember it. They were different people now and all she had to do was to pretend, just for today, that they'd only just met, had just fallen in love.

Tomorrow would be soon enough to get back to

normal, to get on with the life she knew and could rely on.

'Fine.' Black eyes glinted wickedly as he took her hand. 'I'm ready for the afters whenever you say the word. Let's get the "begin with" over.'

They were still holding hands as they wandered slowly beneath the cool green canopy, taking the rarely trodden paths, the only sound that of their feet in the undergrowth, the music of birdsong and the ever-present murmur of the stream.

Idyllic, Caroline thought, or at least it should have been. But it wasn't working. Every step brought back memories of that long-ago summer when she'd believed she'd met her soul mate, when she would have trusted him with her life. How could she divorce herself from the reality of his callous betrayal?

'I've got something I want to show you,' he said as they emerged into a clearing on the banks of the stream. 'Remember Ma's falling down rented cottage?'

Seemingly oblivious of her now sombre mood, he strode ahead of her, holding back the branches of a hazel, his boyish grin lighting his face.

She had no option but to follow, her heart sinking as she recalled that dreadful day. It had taken her a while for everything to sink in. Her father had paid him to go away and stay away. Maggie Pope had confirmed that he was the father of her baby, had confirmed that he'd shrugged, had laid all the responsibility on her and had swaggered away.

So she'd written that letter, in case he'd already

left the area, and it had been easy. All the hurt and bitterness had spilled out onto the paper. And of course he'd already gone.

'Not here,' his austere-featured mother had answered her enquiry. So Caroline had pushed the sealed envelope into her hands. 'Then, give him this if and when you see him again.'

Now the cottage had been transformed, she registered numbly. Before, it had been barely habitable, the extensive garden filled with the produce Mrs Dexter had grown to sell and which had remained unsold. Now the stonework was sturdy, the leaking roof re-thatched and a sizeable, sympathetic extension added, an extension so well executed it might always have been here.

'Well, what do you think?' Ben turned to her, tucking an arm around her, pulling her close to his side.

Caroline pulled away, her features pale and serious. So much for their precious stolen day, for pretending they had no shared past. 'Does your mother still live here?' she asked dully.

The cottage didn't look lived in and the once productive garden was a jungle of weeds, so she didn't think she did. She sighed heavily. She'd tried so hard to block out thoughts of his past betrayal, just for this one day, but being here had made that impossible. 'She never did like me.'

'She was afraid of you,' Ben commented lightly as he took a door key from the pocket of the stone-coloured jeans he was wearing. 'She knew how I felt about you and kept telling me it would all end in tears!' He had opened the carefully restored oak-plank door and it swung back easily on its hinges. 'She was always telling me that the young lady from the big house would never settle down with the local tearaway who had a bad reputation and even worse prospects!'

He loomed over her and Caroline felt something wither and die inside her as he traced the line of her cheek with a caressing forefinger and added gently, 'You didn't ditch me out of snobbishness, Caro. But because of your upbringing you were unable to make a long-term commitment, I understand that now. And you were very young.'

He had been young at the time, too. And sooner or later he would have abandoned her as he'd abandoned Maggie and their baby; sooner rather than later if her father had demanded the return of that money because, typically, he hadn't kept his side of their bargain. Yet he was talking as if she had been the one to blame for everything that had happened.

Ben put a hand beneath her elbow, urging her over the threshold and as if he sensed her resistance he said lightly, 'To answer your question, Ma now lives with her sister Jane in Derbyshire on what used to be the family farm. The land was sold off when their parents died within six months of each other around five years ago. They share the farmhouse.'

They were in the main living room and it seemed much larger and lighter than it had been on the only occasion she'd set foot inside the cottage. Her eyes must have been showing her bemusement because Ben told her, 'When Ma and I lived here, this room was divided by a hardboard partition. She slept behind it and I had a room upstairs with crumbling floorboards and a leaking ceiling.'

So there was light coming from two windows now, and lots more space. The rusty old cooking range had been taken out, revealing a wide inglenook where logs would blaze in the winter. The overhead beams had been cleaned of their peeling layers of black paint and were their warm natural colour.

'The place was a pigsty when we lived here,' Ben confided. 'But because of that the rent was low. We couldn't afford any better.' He had drawn her to the deep window-seat at the far side of the room and she had let him, reluctantly, too low-spirited now to argue. 'You would have seen her around after we came to live here but you never knew her. I think you should. I'm sure you'll get on like a house on fire when you get to know each other properly.'

He had taken her unresisting hand and they were sitting close in the confined space but Caroline didn't feel anything. Just numb.

'People thought she was hard, unfriendly,' he admitted. 'But that was simply a defence mechanism. She called herself Mrs Dexter but she was never married. She simply allowed people to think she was widowed or divorced.

'My father worked with a travelling fair. She and Jane, the sister she was closest to, had sneaked away to the forbidden and ''wicked'' fairground when it first arrived. That was where she met him. A week later they all packed up and moved on and a few weeks on she found she was pregnant.

'Her parents didn't throw her out but they made life uncomfortable. They were devout members of a narrow religious sect and made no secret of the fact that she had shamed them. She stuck it out until I was two.'

He gave her a wry, sideways smile. 'By then she'd stopped waiting for the fair and the man who'd fathered me to return to the area. So she cut her losses and took off and supported me by taking what work she could. We had a settled period in Manchester—I guess it would be around eight years. Then we moved down south and ended up here.

'She had a tough life but she never let it get her down.'

It must have been hard for both of them, Caroline conceded silently. Ben's father had seduced a young girl and had moved away, never giving her another thought. Like father like son? But then, his father hadn't known he'd sired a child.

Ben had. And still he'd walked away.

She shifted uncomfortably on the window-seat. She felt utterly drained and very slightly nauseous. What a fool she'd been to imagine that they could share just one perfect day.

Ben's fingers tightened around hers as he sprang lithely to his feet, his smile radiant with enthusiasm as he invited, 'Come and see the rest—I originally had it restored and enlarged for Ma but she tells me she's settled up north with Jane. If you like it, I could give up my suite at the house—there'd be room for more children if I did—and we could use the cottage when I visit. Or—' his smile deepened to a grin '—if you prefer motherhood and country living over a career in the city, we could make this our permanent home and keep my London apartment on for when we fancy a dose of the bright lights. It's entirely up to you, sweetheart.'

Caroline caught her breath. In this light, completely relaxed mood he was damned near irresistible. She shuddered as a cold wash of misery swamped her. He was obviously taking her acceptance of his proposal for granted after the way she'd turned to him in the night.

It was tempting, more tempting than she wanted to admit, but how could she trust him? She'd trusted him before and look where that had got her. She'd be a fool to fall into the same trap twice,

'Sweetheart?' The question in his voice, the way he probed her eyes as if he were looking deep inside her soul, unglued her tongue.

She stepped away from him, folding her arms around her body and told him sombrely, 'We can't divorce the past from the present, pretend it never happened. You can't, either. The very fact that you brought me here when you'd said we wouldn't give it, or the future, headroom today, proves it.'

'I know what I said.' His tone was serious now, his eyes narrowing as he moved closer again and stroked with the tip of one finger the tiny frown line that had appeared between her eyes. 'I was wrong. We can't forget the way we were, what we had, any more than we can ignore the future.' His hand dropped as he traced the delicate line from the arc of her slanting cheekbone to the angle of her jaw. 'And as for today, right here and now, we're the bridge that connects the two.'

She pulled in a sharp breath, her eyes holding his. They had no future. 'I have thought it over—' Her voice failed but under the pressure of his still narrow-eyed scrutiny she found it again. 'Your proposal, that is. Ben, I can't marry you.'

CHAPTER NINE

FOR long seconds Ben simply looked at her, his features stony. Then he asked rawly, 'So what was last night all about?' His mouth thinned. 'And let's not forget this morning. Just sex was it? Not used to going without and I was handy?'

'No!' Caroline's sharp denial was filled with pain. She couldn't let him think that of her, but she couldn't confess she still loved him. If she did that then the pressure he would put on her to take their relationship into the future, make it as permanent as he wanted it to be, would be intolerable.

It was time for the truth, to be as honest as she could be without revealing the depth of her feelings for him. She gave an involuntary shudder but her lush mouth was firm as she told him. 'When we're together it's as if nothing else matters, as if the rest of the world doesn't exist. It was always like that for me, I admit that freely. And if I could keep it like that, then believe me I would.'

She turned her back on him because she simply couldn't bear to see the eyes that had revealed so many things about him—humour, caring, passion—turning to slits of cold, hard jet.

And there would be worse, she knew that, when she'd explained her position. No man who had created a fortune, his company an international byword, his name highly respected in both business and social spheres, would like to be reminded of his cheating past.

Her eyes on the tangled garden, her heart gave a pain-filled judder. With a lot of hard work and a great deal of pleasure it could be turned into a place of riotous beauty. But of course she would not be the one to make the transformation.

She flicked her tongue over dry-as-dust lips and tried to ease the tension from her shoulders. But it wouldn't go and she forced out thickly, 'After the way you betrayed us all I could never really trust you. I might want and—' she bit off the words, love you, and substituted, '—find you attractive, but I wouldn't trust you not to do the same again.'

'Ah. So we're back to that word betrayal again.'

She heard him move closer, his feet making very little sound on the wide oak boards. She wondered if he'd touch her, but he didn't.

'You were about to tell me what you meant last night, but events overtook us, as I remember.' There was a firm edge of determination in his voice. 'So spit it out now, Caro.'

'Look I know it was a long time ago,' she said tiredly. 'You were young, unprincipled and wild. You might be twelve years older now, successful, extremely wealthy and respected, but people don't change, not basically.'

'Cut to the chase,' Ben instructed, his voice a warning, and she dragged in a breath, wondering why she had to be so stubborn, why she had to be so darned particular. Couldn't she have at least tried to wipe the slate clean, take as much happiness as she could for as long as it lasted?

But trust was important. Too important to be brushed aside as if it didn't matter.

She swallowed to ease the tightness in her throat and stiffened her already tense shoulders. Start with the easy one, the sin he'd already put his hand up for, she told herself.

'My father paid you to go away and stay away. That was bad enough, showed how much I really meant to you. But you went back on the deal, on your own admission. You came panting back to ask me if I was going to marry Jeremy Curtis. I guess your ego couldn't stand the thought that I might have used you the way you'd used me. You went back on that mercenary deal you made with my father. That shows a complete lack of moral integrity.'

A few beats of silence followed, fraught with menace. Caroline felt the hairs on the back of her neck stand on end. She turned swiftly, facing him, just as he snapped out, 'Your father offered me money but I didn't take it. I told him what he could do with it. I didn't renege on any bargain because none was made. If he told you differently, he lied, just as, apparently, he lied when he informed me you were only a couple of months away from announcing your engagement.'

She dropped her lashes. The dark, accusatory glitter of his eyes hurt so much.

'Had you so little faith in me?' Ben demanded heavily. 'I've already explained why I had to head to London at a moment's notice, how I couldn't wait to get back to hear your side of the engagement story. Couldn't you have done the same? Waited to hear what I had to say? Why take your father's word as gospel, write me off?'

Put like that, he had every reason to look so quietly, forbiddingly angry, she acknowledged miserably.

And if the alleged exchange of money for a promise had been the only thing she'd had to worry about at that time then everything would have been different. She would have waited at Langley Hayes to see if he did come back and would have asked him if what her father had said was true.

But it hadn't been the only thing, had it?

'There was more to it than that. I know what you did to Maggie Pope and your baby daughter.' She could hardly get the words out, the memory of the shattering blow she'd endured still had the power to hurt and appall her.

She drew in a deep, ragged breath and said heavily, 'When my father told me I didn't want to believe it. But Maggie confirmed it. You got her pregnant but refused to take any responsibility. You washed your hands of both of them; you didn't want to know. And turned your attention to your next willing victim. Me.'

She watched the colour drain from his face and flinched. The truth hurt, didn't it just. Strangely, she ached to touch him, to make her peace with him. Love, she supposed, was responsible for this almost primal urge to offer comfort. When it came to the crunch love forgave everything, she acknowledged with a tremor of shock.

Instinctively, she reached out a hand but he shook his head abruptly and walked to the door, his voice tight as he bit out, 'I have never touched Maggie Pope, much less fathered a child on her. You have to make a choice whether or not to believe me.' He swung round, his black eyes impaling her. 'In the end, it all comes down to trust, doesn't it?'

The brisk walk back through the woods was accomplished in a silence so intense it set Caroline's nerve ends jangling and made her mouth run dry.

She wanted to tell him she couldn't condone what he'd done but she did understand. He'd been young, highly sexed and his father had set him a terrible example. And maybe, just maybe, he'd been living up to his own reputation as the village Lothario.

She wanted to beg him not to lie about it, especially not to her, not after the passion they'd shared. She wanted to suggest he made amends by getting to know his daughter, helping to provide for her.

Perhaps, that way, they could finally put the past behind them and go on…

The pace he'd set had made her breathless and her voice snagged as she began, 'Ben—listen—please don't lie to me—'

But he cut her short with one slashing movement

of his hand. Scornful eyes stabbed into hers. 'I have *never* lied to you. I suggest you start listening to your heart instead of your cold, judgmental brain. And while you're doing that, you can finish up your work here.' He pulled his lips back against his teeth in a humourless smile. 'You might not have the time, or the inclination, when I'm through thrashing things out with you.'

Stung by his dictatorial, contemptuous tone, hurt by his refusal to trust her enough to admit he'd lied, she glared at him with tear-glittered eyes.

Ben swung round and stalked away, his stride long and rangy as he crossed the gravelled forecourt of Langley Hayes, his aggrieved pride showing in the tense set of his shoulders.

'Wait!' she cried, finding her voice, her tone every bit as dictatorial as his had been. But to her teeth-grinding chagrin he ignored her, striding to his car, gunning the powerful engine, wide tyres scattering gravel as he drove away.

Caroline gritted her teeth and stumped back into the house. The man was impossible. Was his ego so huge he couldn't face humbling himself, admitting he'd done wrong? Did he have to lie about it?

Did he take her for a total fool?

Because twelve years ago Maggie Pope couldn't have been lying. The girl, only a few months older than Caroline herself, would have had no possible reason to tell lies about the identity of her tiny baby's father.

The perfect day she'd planned—they had both

planned—had turned into a nightmare and there would be no going back, no reclamation of the stolen hours that had seemed so enticing earlier on.

Which was possibly just as well, she consoled herself crossly, hoping that if she whipped up enough anger then the heat of it would counteract the icy pain in her heart. It might have been twenty-four hours of paradise, but it would have been a paradise for blind fools.

The phone was ringing as she headed across the hall. Frowning, she decided to ignore it then rapidly changed her mind. It might be one of the contractors Ben had hired to reinvent the estate, and she wasn't going to emulate him and throw a tantrum, regardless of normal everyday duties, nor storm off in a huff!

She took the call in the room that had been her father's study and such was her jagged emotional state it was a full sixty seconds before she registered the identity of the caller.

'Michael,' she responded shortly.

'The one and only! Listen, Caroline, I'm in the area—a big-house sale just outside Shrewsbury. If you're finished up your end, and as hacked off as you sound, you could come back to London with me. Yes?'

She had no further excuse for staying here but the mere thought of leaving Ben, putting their bittersweet reunion behind her, was like the pain of a thousand knives twisting in her heart.

But it had to be done.

'Yes?' Her boss's son repeated his query. 'I say, are you still there, Caroline?'

'Sorry—just thinking.' She pulled in a breath and went on more firmly, 'I've done all that could be done here.'

'Great! I should be with you around four. We can stop off for something to eat on the way…' his voice lowered huskily '…and continue the conversation we were having before you had to go away. *Ciao*, sweetheart!'

She flinched at the endearment Ben had used so effectively during the last twenty-four hours, sounding as if he'd really meant it, and replaced the receiver with unsteady hands. She didn't want any other man to call her sweetheart. She didn't want any other man, full stop.

And what conversation had Michael been referring to? The getting-to-know-each-other-better one, she supposed with a spurt of misery. Remembering her almost clinical detachment at the time when she'd vaguely supposed that her friendly relationship with Michael Weinberg was worth exploring further, she grimaced. How objectively she'd weighed up the pros and cons: to remain single or form a relationship and a family.

It would never happen for her. There was nothing wrong with Michael: he was intelligent, nice-looking, they had much in common. But like the few other men she'd dated during the past twelve years, he wasn't Ben.

Caroline put her fingertips to her aching temples,

her glossy head bowed. Right from the start, all those years ago, Ben had spoiled her for any other man. She dragged her lower lip between her teeth, her breath burning in her lungs.

Hadn't he admitted it had been exactly the same for him? Confessed to having brought her back to Langley Hayes with the intention of finally laying those memories they had of each other to rest, proving beyond any shadow of doubt that what they'd had was nothing special?

And hadn't he admitted frankly that it hadn't worked that way? And what had he told her? She pushed her jumbled hair away from her face. 'I suggest you start listening to your heart.'

As he'd listened to his when he'd excused the hateful letter she'd left with his mother just hours before she'd left this house for good. Excusing it, putting it down to a seventeen-year-old's panicky reaction against making a serious commitment. He'd been wrong, of course, but he had been trying to understand and make allowances because there had been love in his heart and he'd listened to it?

Could she have misjudged him?

Something sweet, a tender fledgling certainty, blossomed in her own heart. Maybe he hadn't driven away in the middle of a temper tantrum, furious because he'd been shown up as far less than perfect. But had gone because he'd needed time on his own to figure out how he was going to convince her he'd been telling the truth.

Caroline walked from the room, closing the door quietly behind her, her mind made up now.

She could readily accept that her father had lied about Ben accepting that pay-off. He would have done anything, said anything, to break up their affair, put a stop to it before Jeremy Curtis got to hear of it. His plans for marrying her off into a wealthy family would have been put in jeopardy.

That left Maggie Pope.

Letting herself out of the house Caroline noted that dull grey clouds had covered the sun, the fickle English spring veering back to winter. She shivered, but began a brisk walk into the village.

There was plenty of time before Michael arrived to collect her to find Maggie and demand the truth. Provided she hadn't left the area.

But that wasn't likely. Her widower father kept the village pub, as his father and grandfather had before him, and Maggie had helped out ever since she'd left school the minute she'd reached sixteen. Continuing to live and work there would be the ideal answer for a single mother with no qualifications.

Even as a chilling wind blew out of nowhere, Caroline's heart sang and she listened. Ben hadn't lied, he wasn't callous now—witness his plans for Langley Hayes—and he hadn't been callous when she'd first known him and had fallen in love with him.

Ben had wanted to marry her way back then and he wanted to marry her now! And they wouldn't have wasted twelve long years if she'd been more mature, refusing to believe those lies until she'd talked to him and had heard what he'd had to say, keeping her faith in him despite her father's insistence that he'd gone for good.

Vowing she'd make it up to him, she lengthened her stride, hugging the hedgerows for protection from the increasingly steady drizzle.

The only enigma was why Maggie had lied. Out of spite? Because the wild, sexy Ben Dexter had never touched her and she'd wished he would?

Caroline had known of his reputation, who hadn't? Sometimes, home from boarding school for the holidays, she'd visited the general store, had heard a group of village girls drooling over the hunky Ben Dexter, giggling and preening if he'd happened to roar by on the old motorbike he'd used to get around on, some of them boasting that they'd ridden pillion with him, implying a whole lot more.

Had Maggie been jealous because she hadn't been one of the lucky ones? Deciding to get her own back by telling everyone that she had?

Whatever. Speculation was getting her nowhere. She had to have the truth, discover what had lain behind the lie that had done so much damage, and she knew she was going to have to wait a short while longer when the heavens opened as she reached the outskirts of the village.

Scurrying, her head down, she headed for the store where she could shelter until the worst had passed.

A violent tapping on a window-pane had her skidding to a standstill.

Dorothy Skeet beckoned her frantically and Caroline dived thankfully under the porch of the pretty cottage and pushed on the open front door.

'You've got drenched!' Dorothy clucked as she emerged from a door on the right. 'I saw you coming down the lane—you can see everything from my front window—and I said to myself, Poor Miss Caroline will get a right soaking! Now, come and dry off by the fire and I'll get you a towel for your hair. And what about a cup of tea? I could fancy one myself.'

Acquiescing gratefully, Caroline entered a cosy, cluttered room and rough-dried her hair in front of the fire that crackled in the tiny hearth while Dorothy went to make the promised tea.

'You've made it very comfortable,' she remarked when the older woman returned with a tray of tea things. 'You're happy here?'

Her father's death must have hit Dorothy hard. She'd lost the man who'd been the centre of her narrow life for years, had lost her home and her livelihood. Caroline felt a nagging sense of responsibility. If Dorothy was having difficulty making ends meet—the legacy wouldn't have amounted to much after her father's debts had been paid—then something would have to be done about it.

'Oh, yes.' Dorothy filled two cups from the squat brown teapot, handing one to Caroline who had put the damp towel aside and was watching the steam rise from her borrowed jeans. 'I miss your dad, of course I do, and I thought I'd be lonely, but I'm not really. There's always someone to talk to and, like I said, I can see all the comings and goings from my window.'

And report them, innocuous or not, to the first willing ear she happened to come across, Caroline thought with a wry smile as she refused the sugar bowl. She probed gently, 'I know you won't be pensionable age, Dorothy. So how are you managing? Don't be afraid to say if you're not. I'll probably be able to help.'

'Bless you, I'm managing fine.' The other woman sank into a roomy armchair, beaming. 'When Mr Dexter's company took over the house he explained why he couldn't keep me on, not as full-time housekeeper anyway. He needs someone young and streetwise to keep up with all those energetic young tearaways he's going to take in. But as soon as the first lot arrives I'm to go there for a few hours each day and just help out here and there, get to know them, be a sort of temporary granny, he said. And until they do arrive he pays me a handsome retainer.' She stirred her tea reflectively. 'He's a good man, that.'

Of course he was, Caroline conceded silently, a lump in her throat. The best. So why had it taken her so long to admit it to herself? She'd been so intent on clinging to the misconceptions of the past that she'd been blinded to the truth.

Her father hadn't been able to love her. So had she, subconsciously, believed that, because he couldn't love her, no one else could, either?

Was that why she'd so easily believed the lies

about Ben, convinced in the dark, hidden parts of her mind that he had never loved her, had merely used her?

She set her empty cup down and rubbed at the frown that had appeared between her eyes. She wasn't into self-analysis. Up until now her thoughts had run in a straight line—no looking back—mapping out her life, building her career, seeing things as black or white, no shades in between acceptable.

Huffing out a breath, she smiled for Dorothy, glancing at the window. She wouldn't be going in search of Maggie now; let her keep her secret. There was no point in hurling recriminations for the damage that had been done in the past. Caroline had to look to the future, the possibility of sharing it with Ben because she knew now that he hadn't lied when he'd stated categorically that he had never touched Maggie Pope.

She said briskly, 'I think the rain's stopped.'

She went to investigate and Dorothy joined her at the window. 'Yes, you're right. But you don't have to rush off, do you?'

'Afraid so.' She grimaced at her crumpled, borrowed clothes. 'I have to get back and change.' Michael was coming at four, but hopefully she wouldn't be leaving with him. She had to see Ben, retract all the hurtful things she'd said, ask him to forgive her and tell him she loved him.

A watery sun was turning the raindrops on the grass of the village green to sparkling diamonds and from where she was standing she could see the picturesque but shabby Poacher's Arms. And partly hidden by the stand of trees in the centre of the green the sleek profile of a Jaguar. Ben's?

As if in answer to her unspoken question the main door opened and Ben strode out, his face grim, followed closely by Maggie, her blonde hair tousled as if she'd been trying to pull it out by the roots, her eyes red and puffy.

And then, dancing around the adults, a tall, coltish child, dark plaits flying around her animated face.

'Maggie's child.'

Caroline hadn't realised she'd spoken the instinctive words aloud until Dorothy confirmed, 'That's right. She'll have grown a bit since you were last here! Gone twelve now, she is. Angela, they call her—though she's no angel—up to every mischief she can find! She's the image of her dad, though, don't you think?'

The giant hand that squeezed her heart made Caroline feel nauseous. The dark braids were a shade or two lighter than Ben's raven hair, but the wiry, coltish grace, the half-tamed joy of living that animated the lively face…

Caroline couldn't answer but Dorothy didn't need confirmation of her remark, her voice avid with her love of gossip as she said, 'Wild horses wouldn't make him admit he's Angie's father but everyone knows it. They've been caught at it, if you take my meaning, more than once. He'd never marry her and make the kid legitimate, of course. Our Maggie's too far beneath him. Well, she's slow on the uptake…'

Dorothy tapped the side of her head meaningfully '...a bit rough and ready, so he wouldn't tie himself to the likes of her. You know him well enough to see that, what with his position and everything.'

Caroline bit down hard on her bottom lip. She desperately wanted to make her excuses and leave but she couldn't move.

Rooted to the spot, she saw Ben grin as he said something to the child, dig in the pocket of his jeans and count coins out into the small, outstretched palm. Watched the little girl skip across the green towards the store, watched Ben turn back to Maggie, his face frigidly serious now.

And Dorothy droned on, oblivious to Caroline's turmoil, 'Mind you, he visits now and then, I'll say that for him. You can see him come and go out of opening hours, usually this time of day. Probably helps out a bit financially, I wouldn't know. But so he should, he's not short of a bob or two, as you know.'

Caroline caught her breath as the hand around her heart squeezed tighter but she managed to uproot her feet from the floor, unglue her tongue from the roof of her mouth, rasping, 'Sorry, I really must go.'

To get away from the words that were drilling holes in her head.

'Must you?' As always, Dorothy Skeet was enjoying her gossip. She dipped her head towards Ben, his face emphatic as he spoke to Maggie. 'Mr Dexter can give you a lift back when he's ready.'

'No!' The negative was torn from her. She turned and fled.

CHAPTER TEN

CLEARING the sharp bend in the narrow lane which put her safely out of sight of the entire village and Dorothy's no doubt astonished eyes, Caroline stopped to catch her breath and let her thumping heartbeats settle down to a more sedate pace, her silky, fine dark brows pulling together in an exasperated frown.

She was doing it again, wasn't she? Running away just as she'd done twelve years ago. Assuming the worst about the man she loved without stopping to hear his side of the story.

Dorothy's opinions weren't conclusive evidence, were they? Opinions formed by village gossips, who had nothing better to do with their time than speculate, elaborate and embroider on the doings of others, weren't to be taken as gospel truth.

And she, Caroline, wasn't going to make the same mistake twice. She would speak to Ben, tell him what Dorothy had said—implied—and listen to what he had to say with an open, trusting mind.

Briefly debating whether to retrace her steps, head back to the village and find Ben or flag him down if he happened to pass her on his way back to Langley Hayes, she glanced down at her wrist-watch.

In just under an hour Michael would arrive to pick

her up so it would probably be better—less of a half-way-to-hysterical impulse—if she carried on up to the house, got cleaned up and changed so that when Ben turned up she could face him with some dignity and poise.

Looking as she did, her hair hanging in straggly rats' tails, her blouse crumpled and the borrowed, too wide, too short jeans still damp and spattered with mud, she must look like a particularly unappealing tramp.

She would have time for a quick shower, she decided as she walked on up the lane trying to avoid the puddles and the rainwater that dripped off the overhanging trees. She'd probably change into the suit she'd arrived in, blow dry her hair and—

She cut her thoughts off with a muffled groan, aware of what she was doing—filling her mind with unimportant trivia to crowd out the terrible doubts.

That he had lied to her and would go on lying.

That the things Dorothy had said were the truth, that everyone knew he was the father of Maggie's child.

She didn't want to have doubts about him, she really didn't, she didn't want them festering in her mind so she'd been trying to blot them out.

She wanted to recapture that earlier faith, the blossoming of certainty that had filled her heart with such sweet joy.

Her throat tightened and thickened with tears as she turned into the Langley Hayes' driveway and walked on towards the house. After what she'd seen and had heard, that earlier certainty was impossible to recapture, but she wouldn't let herself dwell on these negative thoughts before she'd heard what he had to say.

The final bend in the drive brought her in sight of the house and of Michael's blue BMW. Caroline bit back a groan of stark annoyance. Her employer's son was leaning against the bonnet, perfectly relaxed, his legs crossed at the ankles, the hem of his pale green shirt coming adrift from the waistband of his crumpled grey chinos.

She would have much preferred him to be late rather than early. She was going to have to tell him that she couldn't leave until she'd talked to Ben, that he could go on without her and she'd make her own way back to base.

Reluctantly, she returned his wave of greeting and he levered his stocky body away from the car and walked to meet her. His hazel eyes crinkled with laughter as he threw an arm around her shoulders.

'You're early.' Caroline heard the accusatory tone in her voice and tried to moderate it. None of this was his fault. 'I have to—'

No need to go on, the crunch of tyres on gravel told her that Ben had returned. The big car slowed as it drew level. She saw one comprehensive look from narrowed black eyes as Michael grinned and hugged her just that little bit closer, 'What have you done to yourself, my darling? You look more like a scarecrow than my beautiful, elegant partner!'

She wasn't his partner in any sense of the word;

she was his colleague. She fumed inwardly, impatiently shrugging his arm from her shoulder and tucking a straggle of hair behind her ear as Ben shot her a fulminating glare then gunned the engine and ended up parking beside the BMW in a shower of gravel.

Caroline surged forward, her jaw at a determined angle, but Michael captured her waist in what felt like a grip of iron. 'Hang on, what's the rush?'

'I need to speak to Ben—Mr Dexter—'

'Fine. I'm in no hurry, and he doesn't seem to be going anywhere.'

He wasn't. He was waiting. Feet apart, his extravagantly handsome features austere. Caroline's stomach clenched as her heart turned over. The force of his anger was almost visible. She had never, ever, seen him look quite so forbidding.

But Michael seemed blithely unaware of it as they approached the waiting man. His hand outstretched, he acknowledged, 'Dexter—good to meet the guy who gave my find a home!' And at Ben's blank, tight-lipped stare, he elaborated. '*First Love*—the find of the decade.'

Eliciting no response he belatedly introduced himself. 'Michael Weinberg. Caroline told me on the phone that she's finished up here and I offered to drive her back. I'm a tad earlier than I said I'd be, but that's probably a bonus, because I get the impression she's anxious to get under way.'

He turned smiling eyes back to her, and to her ears his voice sounded decidedly intimate. 'We'll stop off for an early supper. I got on the mobile and booked a table at a rather good restaurant just outside Banbury—it will go some way towards making up for the dinner date we had to cancel when you came up here.'

Only when his hand gave a proprietorial squeeze did Caroline become aware that he still had an arm around her waist. Michael was giving entirely the wrong impression. About everything. Wanting to slap a hand over his mouth to stop him saying another word she felt herself redden with frustration then go cold all over as Ben turned contemptuous, half-hooded eyes on her for a long, blistering second before turning back to the other man.

'Yes. I see now.' His voice was flat, the pent-up anger disappearing, making him seem weary. He made a gesture with one hand towards the house. 'Perhaps you'd like to wait inside, Weinberg? I'm sure it won't take Miss Harvey too long to make herself beautiful for you. And would you like her to make you some tea to drink while you wait?'

All cool urbanity now, and then some. Caroline fumed as she escaped Michael's clutches and stalked ahead of them into the house. Ben was savagely angry with her, that much was obvious. Less obvious was the reason.

Because she'd as good as called him a liar, impugned his integrity?

Because, from the way Michael had put it, he'd made it sound as if she'd contacted him and had begged him to fetch her away?

Or because of Michael's overfamiliarity, the way he'd spoken to and about her, his arm possessively around her waist?

Or an explosive combination of all three?

That seemed more than likely and, looking at it that way, she couldn't blame Ben for being so angry, she decided glumly as she walked through to the kitchen to make that dratted tea. They both had a lot of explaining to do. But was he in any mood to listen to anything she said? she questioned, her nerves beginning to shred.

Wondering whether to ask him for ten minutes of his time before she showered and changed, or afterwards when she'd look less messy and ridiculous and just might feel more in control of emotions that were getting more dangerously unstable by the moment, she filled the electric kettle and plugged it in.

Assembling the tea things on a tray was almost impossible, her hands were shaking so much. One of the cups slithered from her fingers and shattered on the tiled floor, when Ben walked in and shouldered the door shut behind him.

The silence after she'd muttered something distinctly unladylike was intense, prickly, painful. A silent accusation hanging in the air, so many things to be said, retracted, so many questions to be asked.

Feeling gauche and incredibly clumsy, tongue-tied because there were so many things to be said and she didn't for the life of her know where to start, Caroline hunted for the dustpan and brush, found it eventually and swept up the mess.

And all the time he said nothing, watching her with those cold, narrowed eyes. The kettle was boiling furiously as she tipped the shards into the waste bin.

At least the question of when they would talk had been taken out of her hands. It was Ben who broke the silence that was making her feel like a halfwit on the edge of hysteria as he went to deal with the kettle, pour the boiling water onto the leaves she'd already spooned into the pot. 'If you'd been ready to leave with your gallant rescuer before I got back, would you have left me another Dear John letter, I wonder?'

He arranged the milk jug and sugar bowl on the tray with neat precision, his hands perfectly steady, his voice like an arctic night as he answered his own question before she had a chance to make any reply, 'No, I suppose you wouldn't. As your partner has already let slip, you can't wait to get way, you wouldn't have wanted to waste the time putting pen to paper. You'd already told me exactly what you thought of me.'

The tea preparations finished, he picked up the tray and Caroline said tautly, 'I know you're angry, but I'm not feeling too euphoric, either.' She searched his impressive but chilling features for some sign of the closeness they had so recently shared. She found none. So she reminded herself that she was a grown woman of above average intelligence and said emphatically, 'We really do need to talk.'

The look he turned on her said he found her statement completely incomprehensible. His head tilted slightly to one side, he uttered, 'I can't think why, when there's nothing more to say.' He gave a slight, insouciant-seeming shrug. 'But if you insist I'll give you five minutes of my time when you're ready to leave.'

He walked to the door then turned to face her, 'I'll serve tea to your partner while you get your things together. Oh, and just one more thing, I spoke to Maggie Pope this afternoon. She admitted that your father paid her to name me as the father of her child, should you ask.' He gave her a mocking smile that was totally devoid of humour. 'He certainly put the money I refused to take to good use.' His beautifully shaped mouth hardened, 'Not that you'll believe me, of course. That would be too much to ask. You've probably already decided that I somehow twisted her arm to persuade her to say that.'

He left as swiftly and silently as he'd appeared, left before she had time to even begin to respond to what he'd said.

It was the best she could do, Caroline thought as she nervously scanned her reflection half an hour later.

Deciding against the suit she'd arrived in as being too formal, too much like the hard-nosed career woman she'd done her best to portray when she'd arrived here, she'd dressed in a sleek-fitting, beautifully tailored sage green skirt, topped by a lighter toned fine cashmere sweater. But not even her skilled application of make-up could disguise the haunted look in her eyes or the lines of strain around her mouth.

Ben's stress on the word 'partner' told her a lot. He thought her relationship with Michael was much closer than it was. Bleakly she recalled what he'd said earlier when he'd asked her what last night and this morning had been about, implying that she'd been missing regular sex and he'd been handy.

Implying that she was some kind of nymphomaniac!

Michael's words and attitude would have reinforced that rock-bottom opinion.

Casting a final look around the room that had been hers for the first, almost eighteen, years of her life she told herself to think positively.

She loved Ben and, more importantly, she trusted him now, implicitly. What he'd told her about Maggie Pope made perfect sense, made everything else slot into place.

Her father's plan to buy Ben off had failed; so what better way to blacken his character and put an end to what he'd thought was his daughter's infatuation with an unsuitable man than to use the spurned money to pay Maggie to tell those lies?

The girl wasn't too bright and ever since the drink-drive laws her father had barely scraped a living, only the immediate locals using the bar at The Poacher's Arms. Money was tight and Maggie'd had a small baby to care for.

Yes, it did make perfect sense; it was just a pity Ben had been too angry to hang around long enough to hear her tell him she believed every word of what he'd said.

Still, he'd promised they'd talk before she left. They'd work things out; they had to. Then maybe she could stay—unless Ben needed some time to think things over. She loved him so desperately and, even if he hadn't said he still loved her, he did have deep feelings for her. He'd asked her to marry him, to share his life, and he wouldn't have done that if all they had was fantastic sex.

Ben would be waiting. Caroline picked up her bag and walked through the door. A trillion butterflies were performing acrobatics in her stomach.

'That's more like it—well worth waiting for!' Michael's warm hazel eyes swept over her with male approval as he laid the newspaper he'd been reading aside and got to his feet, levering himself out of the deep armchair. 'If you're ready, we'll get moving.' He took her bag from her suddenly nerveless fingers. 'It will be good to have you back at base. I've missed you.'

Caroline ignored that. 'I can't leave yet,' she stated firmly. 'I have to speak to Ben.' She scanned the study, as if expecting to see him emerge from behind the shabby furniture, but only the used tea cups testified that he'd ever been here.

'He's gone,' Michael relayed blithely as he walked to the door. 'No worries—he said to tell you goodbye and thanks.'

Goodbye? A final goodbye? And thanks? For what? A few sessions of out-of-this-world sex?

Her heart plummeted down through the soles of her shoes and the butterflies in her stomach went into panic mode. 'Gone where?' she demanded hoarsely, pattering after Michael as he crossed the main hall.

He'd promised they'd talk before she left. He couldn't have simply gone. Unless he'd been so disillusioned and disgusted by her lack of trust he'd decided he never wanted to have to set eyes on her again, much less to have to listen to her accuse him of being a liar.

Michael shrugged. 'Couldn't say. He said he'd just remembered an appointment and shot out. And we're not to worry about locking up. Apparently he was going to ask the site manager to do it before he leaves this evening.'

This evening? Did that mean she could sit around waiting for him all night and he still wouldn't turn up?

Probably, she conceded numbly. If he really had suddenly remembered an appointment too important to cancel, if he really had wanted to thrash things out with her—as he'd intimated much earlier—then he would have left a different message, something along the lines of getting in touch at a later date.

He'd invented that appointment, she was sure of it, she decided, feeling limp and sick to her stomach. He just couldn't be bothered to argue his case with a woman who'd made it plain what she thought of his morals.

And Michael confirmed it when he joined her in the car. 'Dexter asked me to invoice him for your time, but you're not to bother with an evaluation. He can decide for himself what's worth keeping and what's not.' He fastened his seat belt and turned the key in the ignition. 'I don't know why he wanted you up here in the first place. Still, if he wants to waste his money, that's his affair.' The car drew smoothly away. 'Was there much of interest around the place?'

'Not much.' Automatically, Caroline mentioned the pieces that would be worth keeping as an investment, her mind functioning on a different level entirely.

Was there a hidden meaning behind his statement that he could decide what was worth keeping and what was not? Meaning *she* was not worth keeping?

Probably. But there could be no doubt that his instruction regarding her written evaluation meant he wanted no further contact.

Ben Dexter had washed his hands of her and, looking at the sorry mess from his point of view, she couldn't blame him.

He had finally done what he'd set out to do. Got her out of his system.

CHAPTER ELEVEN

SITTING opposite Michael in the small but elegantly appointed restaurant on the outskirts of Banbury, Caroline wondered miserably how she could ever have imagined that their close and friendly working relationship could have developed into something so very much more. Marriage, home-building, children—leading eventually to a companionable old age.

She would never have been able to love him. How could she love him, or any other man for that matter, when Ben had captured her heart and had never let it go? Michael deserved far better than that.

She stared unseeing at the plate of green salad she'd ordered, bleakly looking into a lonely, loveless future and Michael said, 'Aren't you going to eat that? I must say, it certainly looks pretty boring to me—you should have gone for the duck, it's brilliant.'

'Sorry.' Caroline gave him a wan smile and picked up her fork and speared a dressing-slicked leaf without any enthusiasm. 'I'm tired, I guess.'

Although drained was more like it. Drained of energy and hope. Too listless to have been able to tell Michael she'd much prefer to get straight back to London rather than take an early supper break.

Besides, that would have been selfish. Michael must have been ravenous if the way he'd demolished his meal was anything to go by.

'Tired? What brought that on?' A sandy brow lifted enquiringly as he laid down his cutlery and relaxed back in his chair. 'From the little of real interest you say you found at Langley Hayes, I wouldn't have thought you've been overworked exactly.'

There was no getting around that. It was time to be honest and open, to explain why his suggestion that they get to know each other better on a personal level was a non-starter. She owed Michael that much at least.

Caroline laid down her fork and confessed numbly, 'I don't want this to go any further, but Ben—Mr Dexter—and I go back a long way, Mike. We had an affair twelve years ago. It ended after a couple of months or so. I didn't see him again until he came to look at the Lassoon painting.' She pulled in a breath then went on doggedly. 'The last few days have been pretty traumatic.'

'Good God!' He looked stunned. He stared at her for long, assessing moments then stated bluntly, 'You're still in love with him, aren't you?'

Her throat too tight to allow her to speak, Caroline nodded and Michael said slowly, 'If it's lasted that length of time, with nothing to feed on, it has to be the real thing.' He gave her a twisted smile. 'I guess that puts me right out of the frame.' He lifted his shoulders then slowly let them drop. 'But then, I don't suppose I was ever really in it, was I? And you were too polite to tell me. Still friends, though?'

'Of course,' she answered, on a rush of gratitude, glad he was taking it like this, even more relieved to know that his feelings hadn't taken a thorough battering. As hers had done. She wouldn't wish that on her worst enemy.

But she wasn't going to think of that, of bruised and battered feelings; she wouldn't let herself. If she allowed herself to think of what she had almost had and thrown away with her lack of trust, she would put back her head and howl like a dog and embarrass both of them. But then Michael asked, 'Does he feel the same?'

An iron fist clenched around her heart, the pain unbearable, her voice a ragged whisper as she got out, 'Once, perhaps. Not any more.'

'I thought I detected a bit of an atmosphere. Had a fight, did you?'

'Something like that.' She didn't want to say any more on the subject but Michael wouldn't let it go.

He inched towards her, his forearms on the table, his fingers touching hers, just briefly, as he told her, 'He'll get over it—whatever you fought about. Caroline, he isn't a fool. And—' he cleared his throat and added uncomfortably, his face going pink '—I don't know, but I might have put my foot in it. Well, we were talking while we waited for you. He was asking questions, about your position at the gallery, whether you were wedded to your career—that sort of stuff.' He fell silent as their waiter approached to clear the main course and Caroline gave an inner groan of despair.

Had Ben, even at that stage, still wanted to marry her? Why else should he have tried to find out how much her work meant to her? He'd given her a free choice earlier, when he'd made that stunning proposal of marriage: continue with her career, live in London and use the cottage for weekends, or make it their permanent home.

Her throat clogged with tears. She made a determined effort to swallow them. Of course he hadn't still been thinking of marriage. He'd been disgusted by her, by her total lack of trust.

Michael was saying something. Caroline hauled herself out of her pit of misery and said thickly, 'Sorry?'

'I asked if you would like the dessert menu.'

She shook her head, unable at the moment to trust her voice. She couldn't eat, she simply couldn't. She just wanted to get out of here, get back to London and lick her wounds in private.

But Michael had ordered coffee. Caroline smothered a sigh of sheer impatience and Michael mumbled, 'I feel a fool. I had no idea you and he—well, why would I? I'm afraid I gave him the impression you and I were an item. That when Dad retires next year and I take over you'd be a full partner.' His face turned bright red. 'And my wife. Well,' he said brusquely, on the defensive now, 'I did have hopes in that direction, and I guess I was jumping the gun. Over-confidence is my one big failing, or so the old man keeps telling me. Look,' he offered grimly, 'if it'll help heal the rift I'll swallow my pride and call Dexter first thing tomorrow to put him straight.'

'I'd rather you didn't,' Caroline returned stiffly. It was over. Ben had already let her know in no uncertain terms how disgusted he was with her before that conversation had taken place.

The wrong impression Michael had given Ben made her stomach churn queasily but it wasn't anything to make a song and dance about. It would have been nothing more than the final nail in the coffin of their already doomed relationship.

'It wouldn't make a scrap of difference,' she said dismissively with a fatalistic sigh. She looked pointedly at her watch. 'If you're ready, could we make a move? I need a good night's sleep if I'm going to be fit for anything in the morning.'

A good night's sleep was difficult to come by, Caroline decided edgily four weeks later, as she ran a duster over the uncluttered surfaces in her minimally furnished small sitting room.

By armouring herself in designer suits and the mask of her make-up, absorbing herself in her work, she got through the days. And weekends she spent with whichever of her friends happened to be free. But the nights…

The nights were unadulterated torment. Ben took the starring role in dreams that grew ever more sexually explicit and she would come partially awake and reach for him, but he wasn't there, and never would be.

And she'd spend the remaining hours until daylight telling herself that it was over, making herself accept it, facing the fact that Ben would have put their ill-fated relationship firmly behind him, finally ridding himself of her, of his memories of her. Because what man in his right mind could want a woman who openly stated that she didn't trust him?

She was coming dangerously close to hating herself, unravelling round the edges, unable to eat or sleep, tormented by the thoughts of her lost love.

She tossed the duster aside, angry with herself. If her life was a mess she had only herself to blame. So something had to be done about it. And no one else would do it for her.

When Edward Weinberg had said, 'You look dreadful. You're either terminally ill and not telling anyone, or I'm working you too hard. I'm inclined to believe the latter, so take two weeks off. Go to the continent and lie on a beach', she'd wanted to dig her heels in and refuse to do any such thing.

But perhaps the enforced break was just what she really needed to straighten herself out, to do something positive. But what?

Lying on a beach held no appeal. Too much time to think, to brood. She needed hard, physical work.

Casting a look around her sterile living quarters, she made up her mind, grabbed a jacket and walked out.

And two hours later she was back, weighed down

with tins of paint, brushes, fabric swatches, cheap denim jeans and T-shirts from the local street-market.

The apartment she'd previously viewed simply as a place to sleep was going to be turned into a proper home.

'Talk about a sea change!' Danielle Booth, Caroline's neighbour from across the hall, poked her sleek brown head around the open door. 'You've worked your socks off all week so how about a girls' night out—you're not going to work all weekend, I forbid it! You'll give yourself painter's elbow!'

Warm apricot emulsion had transformed the vestibule—formerly an uninspiring pale grey—and the partly open door through to the sitting room revealed the same colour but in a slightly deeper tone.

'Do you like it?' Caroline, on her knees, putting the finishing touches to the skirting board, wanted to know because this was her first attempt at home-decorating and she wasn't sure she'd got it right.

She scrambled to her feet and Danielle said, 'I love it. But I would never have put you down as a hands-on sort of person. Have the decorators in and stay at an hotel until they'd finished would be more your style. And I've never seen you look anything but perfectly groomed before—'

'There's always a first time.' With difficulty Caroline returned her friend's grin. Danielle wasn't to know that she was having to keep herself occupied every minute of her time to stop herself brooding. Over what might have been, over what she had so briefly had and had stupidly thrown away. 'And it's nice not to have to bother about the way I look. Coffee?'

'I'd love some, but I can't. Hair appointment,' Danielle stated. 'Now, what about tonight? We could take in a film, have supper.'

'Sorry,' Caroline declined. She wasn't ready for a relaxed evening out; she'd be terrible company. 'I've got a bedroom to paper. We'll hit the town some other time?'

Danielle planted her hands on her curvaceous hips, her chin going up at an angle as she huffed, 'Caroline Harvey—you are the most stubborn creature—' and fell silent as another, harder voice intervened, 'A sentiment I most sincerely endorse.'

Ben!

Caroline didn't know whether she'd spoken his name aloud or whether it simply rattled around inside her head. In any case, her heart had stopped, she was sure it had. Danielle was staring with wide grey eyes, her mouth partly open, her cheeks flushed.

Caroline could understand that reaction because Ben Dexter was something else: six feet plus of sizzlingly virile masculinity clothed in a silvery grey suit that fitted the lithe body to perfection; dark, dark hair, beautifully groomed, and eyes as black as night, fringed by those extravagant lashes.

And he was still angry, she recognised with a shock of icy sensation that ran right down her spine and all the way back up again. The atmosphere positively thrummed with it, although he cloaked it with the urbanity of the smile he turned on Danielle, who went pinker and burbled, 'Well, I'll be off, then.' And behind Ben's back she rolled her eyes expressively, grinned and gave the stunned Caroline the thumbs-up sign.

'Am I to be invited in?' His voice was all honey-smooth on the surface but quite definitely laced with ice. Caroline put a hand up to where a pulse was beating madly at the base of her throat.

She had dreamed of being with him again, yearning, aching, desperate dreams, but the reality filled her with a deep and dark foreboding. He had the face of an austere stranger. He looked as if what they had been to each other, the glimpses of paradise they'd shared, had been ruthlessly wiped from his memory.

Wordlessly, she stepped aside, her heart flipping over because it was there, and always would be, the fateful, deeply ingrained physical recognition that made her body ache for his.

His taut profile grim, he strode ahead of her into the sitting room, a single raking glance taking in her few pieces of shrouded furniture, the paint-spattered newspapers spread all over the floor. And then his eyes flowed over her, making her suddenly and horribly aware of the sight she must present. Cheap baggy jeans and sloppy T-shirt, liberally splashed with paint, her hair caught back from her make-up-less face with a piece of string.

But the sheer length of his scrutiny, the slow gleam of something sultry in those narrowed black eyes sent her dizzy with hope. Maybe, just maybe, it wasn't dead for him, either.

The violent sexual attraction, the meeting and mating of souls that had lasted through twelve, long years of separation, making them both unfit partners for anyone else on the planet, couldn't have been wiped out overnight. Surely it couldn't.

Her head still swimming, her lower limbs suddenly feeling like cotton wool she forced herself to say something, anything, to break the charged and spikey silence. And the breaking of it would enable him to open up, tell her why he was here when he hadn't wanted to have to talk to her at all on that dreadful last day at Langley Hayes.

'Can I—' her tongue felt as if it were twisted into knots. Her milky skin burned with fierce colour as she forced out the words '—offer you coffee?'

'This isn't a social call.'

His voice was flat, the eyes that pinned hers were hard and dark. His feet planted apart, he pushed his hands into the pockets of his trousers, his superbly cut jacket falling open to reveal the pale grey silk of the shirt that covered the broad plane of his chest. 'It's been long enough—a full month. I used no protection. Although knowing now of your relationship with the younger Weinberg, I guessed you're more than likely to be on the pill.'

His staggeringly handsome features were blank but his eyes brimmed with unconcealed contempt. 'However, I need to know if you're pregnant. And if you are, I need to know if it's mine, or Weinberg's.'

His lips pulled back against his teeth in a smile that wasn't a smile at all. 'Tell me you're not and I'll leave you in peace. And I promise you'll never have to see me again.'

Caroline swayed on her feet, the final frail hope snatched away from her. Her soft mouth trembled as her blood roared in her ears. So much pain coming on the top of all that had gone before. She didn't know how she was going to bear it.

Darkness closed in on her and she felt herself falling.

CHAPTER TWELVE

GRATING out a harsh expletive, Ben's voice sounded as if it were echoing over some vast distance, and his face, hovering over her, was fuzzy, as if the bright May morning had spawned a thick November fog.

Caroline shook her head and her vision cleared; she had to be imagining the sharp stab of concern in the night-black eyes.

Of course he didn't care about her, not any more, and she wasn't going to be pathetic or crazy enough to let herself even begin to hope that he did. If he hadn't been too lost in passion when they'd made love to remember to use protection he wouldn't be here at all, she reminded herself wretchedly.

Struggling to escape the arms that were holding her upright, she gave a strangled, anguished sob. Being held so close to the hard heat of his body was torture, all the more painful because her own body was flooding with a wildfire heat of its own, her pulses racing, her breath coming in shallow gasps.

'Stop it!' His command was rough-edged as he subdued her feeble efforts by sweeping her up into his arms and shouldering his way through doors until he found her bedroom.

With a muted hiss of impatience, Ben swept the rolls of wallpaper off the narrow single bed and lowered her down onto it. 'Stay right there,' he stated emphatically. 'I'll fetch you a glass of water.'

A piercing glance from under lowered brows reinforced her opinion that concern for her well-being had been a product of her own demented imagination, an immature grasping at non-existent straws. He simply and obviously regarded her as nothing more than a nuisance, her unprecedented collapse something he had to handle but could very well have done without.

She turned her face into the pillow and shuddered. She wished he'd go away. It was better to be alone, struggling to accept that everything was finally over, rather than have to see him the way he was now. She didn't want to have to remember him like this, so cold, so contemptuous, so forbidding.

How he must hate her!

'Drink this.'

Unwillingly, Caroline dragged herself up against the pillows, not meeting his eyes. She couldn't bear to see that raw contempt, that stinging impatience.

'You fainted,' he said tonelessly as she clutched the glass in both hands and lifted it shakily to her mouth. 'Women in the early stages of pregnancy often do, so I believe.'

A savage spurt of temper got her kick-started. Colour flooding her ashen face, she swung her legs over the side of the bed, putting the glass on the floor before she gave into the temptation to throw it at him.

Out of a sense of duty he'd come here with the sole purpose of finding out if she was pregnant.

That was chastening.

But he had also come to find out—if her answer was in the affirmative—whether he or Michael was the father.

And that was disgusting, infuriating!

How could he think that of her? Oh, how could he?

'What do you think you're doing?' His question was laced with a good dose of aggravation as he caught hold of her ankles.

And before she could answer, Getting ready to strangle you before I throw you out, he swung her legs back onto the bed and told her, 'You need to rest. You look dreadful.'

Thanks a bunch, Caroline fulminated silently. While he, of course, looked immaculate, remote as the moon, forbidding and utterly, utterly, heart-stoppingly gorgeous. And deserving of some hefty punishment for marking her down as a slut!

'So what will you do if I confirm my pregnancy?' she asked out of sheer wickedness, watching for his reaction beneath lowered lashes.

'Marry you, if it's mine—make sure my child's properly cared for.' Not a flicker of emotion, nothing, just a bland statement of intent.

'And if it's Michael's?' Caroline turned the screw, increased the punishment in an anger-fuelled and completely ignoble attempt to pay him back for his lower-than-low opinion of her.

She saw his jaw clench, a white line of anger appear around his compressed lips, as he ground out between his teeth, 'That would be entirely up to him. Apparently, the poor sucker already thinks he's going to lead you up the aisle. He hasn't yet worked out that you're unable to commit to a long-term relationship.'

The contempt in his eyes deepened. 'When push comes to shove, you back off in a panic, write a Dear John letter or pick one hell of a fight. As I should know. And I somehow doubt if he's got the strength of character to make you toe the line.'

And Ben had?

Of course he had. Commitment to him would never have been a problem; it had been her inability to trust him that had turned everything sour. Her fatal mistake.

Her dark head drooped, her tear-filled eyes fastening on her hands which appeared to be trying to rip the hemline of her paint-spattered T-shirt to shreds.

This had gone far enough.

'I'm definitely not pregnant,' she told him in a voice that was flat and cold and thin. And she closed her heavy eyes and waited to hear the bedroom door shut behind him as he left. He now had the information he must have been desperately hoping to get. There would be nothing to keep him here for one more moment.

She heard nothing, just the silence, until his voice sliced at her, 'Then what the hell was that all about? The "what if it's yours, or what if it's his" spiel?'

Caroline risked a glance beneath the thick sweep of her lashes, her mouth dropping open in astonishment because she'd been so sure he'd stalk straight out the moment he had the reassurance he'd come for.

He still looked coldly, furiously angry. She looked away, her heartbeat thundering in her ears, and she lay back, turning her face into the pillows.

She couldn't stand much more of this. 'I wanted to pay you back for thinking I'd do something like that,' she muttered wearily, her voice scarcely above a whisper. The anger had gone, leaving a sense of loss that utterly overwhelmed her. 'Make love with you while supposedly in a serious relationship with Michael Weinberg.'

'And that made you angry, did it?' The query was laced with something approaching sarcasm. Then Ben's voice thickened, 'Then, you know what it feels like, don't you? Not to be trusted. To have someone you loved think you're capable of every slimey trick in the book.'

'Loved.' Past tense. So final. The door labelled Hope that had remained stubbornly ajar closed with a definitive bang in her mind.

Caroline hauled herself into a sitting position and swung her feet to the floor. Somehow she had to put an end to this nightmare. And she could cope. Right?

She would never forget him but eventually the terrible pain would leave her. The scar tissue on her heart would grow hard, letting her get on with her career because that was all she had, with never a hint that she had once been capable of any kind of emotion.

And she knew what she had to do to get the process started.

She wiped the moisture from her cheeks with fingers still sticky from the paintbrush and said with a calmness that belied all the anguished turmoil inside her, 'You can go now. I'm fine. I don't know why I passed out.' She gave the hint of a tight, impersonal smile, a small hike of one shoulder. 'It's not something I've done before. Probably down to the paint fumes.'

And being unable to eat, nor sleep; and seeing him again, coupled with the brief resurrection of hope and it's inevitable demise. But she certainly wasn't going to mention that.

'Then, perhaps we should open some windows.' And he moved around the flat, doing just that. Caroline got wearily to her feet. When he'd finished he'd leave, nothing surer than that. Her legs felt unsteady and she had to hang onto the door frame when she'd tracked him down in the kitchen.

Please go, she whimpered, in her mind. I need to start the long, slow, agonisingly painful process of getting over you again.

He was taking in the frantic muddle: the opened tins of paint; emulsion brushes soaking in her stainless-steel washing-up bowl; the ones used for gloss paint standing up to their necks in white spirits; the old dusters she'd used to wipe up all the splodges she'd made screwed up on the floor. And the pizza she'd ordered ages ago and hadn't been able to eat because just looking at it had turned her stomach.

'When we met again, that evening, I would have staked my last penny against you ever deigning to get your pretty white hands dirty.'

Which was why he'd taken one look at her, her make-up a perfect mask, not a hair out of place, her designer suit a statement of her status as a cool, efficient career lady, and had sent her to grovel in the dust of the Langley Hayes attics, she thought with a reluctant inner salute for his ability to cut her down to size.

Caroline merely shrugged. It seemed to take the last scrap of energy remaining to her, but she managed to say, 'You can go now.'

Ben ignored her. He turned his back on her, filled the kettle and plugged it in, searching for mugs and tea bags. There was no milk, just a curdled couple of inches in the bottom of a carton. He tossed it into the pedal bin. 'Empty fridge, an untouched pizza wearing a mouldy wig—you certainly know how to look after yourself.'

He moved aside a pile of old newspapers, a roll of masking tape, the ancient pizza, and put two mugs of milkless tea on the small square table. Pulling out two chairs he ordered, 'Sit.'

She complied because it seemed easier than arguing, but she told him, 'There's no need for you to do this—make tea, hang around. I can look after myself.'

'Obviously!' His tone was dry. Then, his voice

lower, gruffer, he admitted, 'I don't like to see you like this—washed out, exhausted.'

His words made her heart contract and twist, but she wasn't going to let herself read anything into them that wasn't there. Lifting her mug in both hands she took a sip of the strong, hot brew and then another, and felt for the first time since he'd walked in on her just a fraction more than half-alive.

Revived enough, she asked the question that had been lodged in the back of her mind. 'Who is the father of Maggie Pope's daughter? Did she tell you?'

'You've already decided I am,' he reminded her brusquely and pushed his mug to one side with an expression of deep distaste. Whether for the milkless tea or for her, she didn't know. The latter, she supposed.

'No.' Her mug had left a damp circle on the surface of the table. She rubbed at it with her forefinger. 'Not now, not after you told me what she'd said, that Dad had paid her to tell that lie. I do admit,' she went on tiredly, 'to believing her twelve years ago, and going on believing her. When he—my father, that is—said he'd given you money to go away and stay away, I couldn't believe it, not of you. I thought you really loved me, the way I loved you.'

A final rub with the heel of her hand and the ring of moisture disappeared. 'Then, of course, came the final blow. He suggested I ask Maggie who had fathered her child. Maybe I shouldn't have done, but think what it was like—I was only seventeen, all churned up emotionally. You'd disappeared, Dad had planted those doubts in my mind. I had to know. Well, you know what she said, and why she said it. She was very convincing.'

Caroline lifted her eyes to find Ben watching her, his burning gaze roving over her face. She felt the muscles in her shoulders relax. Even if he had no strong feelings for her now because her lack of trust had killed them stone dead, it felt good to get it all off her chest.

She pulled in a deep breath. 'That awful day—when I'd said I couldn't marry you because I couldn't trust you—after you drove away I went to see Maggie and get the truth out of her. The real truth,' she stressed. 'You'd told me to listen to my heart, do you remember? And I did. My heart told me you'd been telling the truth, that you were nowhere near callous enough to betray anyone. The only question was, why had Maggie lied? I was going to drag the truth out of her. But it started to pour with rain and I sheltered at Dorothy's. We saw the three of you. Maggie, you and the child. Dorothy was looking at you and talking about the child's father, talking as if I knew him.'

'And that put me back in the frame?'

'Not entirely.' She shook her head. 'I went back to the house to wait for you. Michael had phoned, he was in the area, and was to drive me back. I knew we didn't have much time, I knew we had to talk, and I knew—' she met his eyes, willing him to believe her, '—that I would believe, implicitly, whatever you told me. You were still angry, but you did say we'd talk before I had to leave. But you'd gone when I came down after changing.'

For long, aching minutes he didn't respond, the silence putting her nerve ends on the rack. She stood up jerkily, clearing the mugs for something to do to end this nail-biting stasis and Ben shot to his feet.

Caroline's teeth bit into her lower lip. He was leaving. Her garbled attempt at self-justification, apology, had cut no ice. But then, had she really expected it to, she thought wretchedly. She half turned away and Ben took the mugs from her clenched fingers, dumped them back on the table and pulled her round to face him.

'Jeremy Curtis is Angela's father. Presumably that was why Dorothy was talking as if you knew the man. That's the drill when it comes to serious village gossip—name no names. Simply imply. Don't run the risk of being sued for defamation of character.'

Jeremy? Oh, sweet heavens above! He'd been having an affair with the unsuitable Maggie while her father and his had been planning her own marriage to the Curtis fortune! Jeremy would have gone along with it because she, Caroline, was suitable-wife material and poor Maggie wasn't. It might have been funny if the consequences hadn't been so devastating.

The hands that had gripped her upper arms gentled. His thumbs stroked her skin beneath the sleeves of her T-shirt, hypnotic, holding her immobile, her power of speech wiped out by the hot pressure of emotion building up around her heart.

'It was a shock when I saw you were getting ready to leave, presumably without hanging around long enough to say goodbye,' Ben admitted rawly. 'I'd finally got the truth out of Maggie and I was determined to get you to accept it, trust me enough to be my wife. But I left because I couldn't bear listening to young Weinberg for a moment longer. The things he was saying did my head in. I would have smashed his teeth through the back of his neck if I'd stayed,' he said roughly.

His hands came up to cup her face, his eyes holding hers with an intensity that made her mouth run dry. He murmured, 'Think back, Caro. You said that I'd thought you'd made love with me while you were supposedly in a serious relationship with young Weinberg. Supposedly, being the operative word.'

Caroline drew in a deep, shuddering breath that racked her slender frame. So Michael's laid-back over-confidence had done the damage after all. Ben hadn't washed his hands of her; he'd just gone out to find the truth and would have done his damnedest to make her believe it.

Tears flooded her eyes. The temptation to lay her head against his chest was immense. Resisting it, she said thickly, 'Michael and I always worked well as colleagues, and after his divorce we became friends. Just friends.' Caroline swallowed round the sharp, painful lump in her throat.

Would Ben discount what Michael had said and accept in his heart that she was telling the truth? But why should he, when she had believed the worst of him for so long? It really didn't bear thinking about. 'We have never been more than colleagues and friends, I promise you.'

She twisted away from him before he could move away from her and thus let her know that what she was saying was very far from convincing. Her slight shoulders slumped, she folded her arms around her body, holding in the misery, the sheer trepidation.

'To be completely honest with you, I did begin to realise that he wanted more than friendship. And because my wretched biological clock had started ticking loudly I even thought that he and I could progress to a closer relationship, given time. Then—then you came back on the scene.'

Her voice snagged in her throat, but she pressed on. 'And I knew it couldn't work, not with Michael, not with any other man. You haunted me. And it wasn't long before I knew I'd never stopped loving you, and never would, despite what I thought you'd done. Michael told me what he'd said to you. He knew something was wrong, and I ended up confessing that I was in love with you. He said he'd put his foot in it—offered to phone the next day and explain he'd jumped the gun. But I thought I was beyond forgiveness.'

One, two, three heartbeats of silence.

Caroline felt her already shaky control begin the tight spiral that would end in explosion and disintegration. And then she felt his hands gently touch her shoulders. She expelled a long, shaky breath of relief and sagged weakly back against him, her eyes drifting shut as his hands lifted to untie the length of string that bound back her hair.

Fanning the dark mass over her shoulders he turned her to face him, his voice unsteady, 'You've got paint in your hair.'

'I know.' Her eyes were dreamy, a misty deep violet. Her hands splayed out against his chest, parting his jacket to find the vital, living warmth of him through the silk of his shirt. 'Probably on my teeth, too.'

'I guess.' He lifted one of her hands and placed a kiss on the inside of her wrist, just where her pulse began a crazy tattoo.

'I look a complete mess.' She found it difficult to speak when her heart was thundering, her body quivering as he pressed the hard span of his hips against hers.

'Do you? I hadn't noticed.' His voice thickened as she captured his hand and pressed fervent, dancing kisses on the back of each finger in turn. 'I just love you.'

He drew in a harsh breath then kissed her with a savage hunger that drew a wild and wanting response from her as she clung to him, the whirlwind of passion making words unnecessary. They were together, just as fate had intended them to be; they were home, soul mates; they understood. They were complete.

She could feel the drum beats of his heart as he lifted her and carried her to the bedroom. Laying her on the top of the duvet he slowly shrugged out of his jacket, his cheekbones flushing darkly as he said,

'I'm going to bind you to me for the rest of my life, love you and care for you for the rest of my life. And I'm going to make love to you, now, with no hidden agendas, no fantasies, just you and me and what we feel for each other.'

His shirt followed his jacket. The dark eyes he kept fixed on her drenched with burning emotion, and Caroline bounced back up, dragged her T-shirt over her head, and held her arms wide for him. 'My darling, come to me, come home…'

The warm, late May sunshine tempted Caroline out of the cottage before she'd even started on the customary morning chores. An internal wriggle of sheer pleasure made her screw her eyes shut and beam, her grin stretching from ear to ear.

The surrounding woods were full of birdsong and the garden was showing promise of becoming as fabulous as she meant it to be. And in two days' time she and Ben would be celebrating their first wedding anniversary.

A year of bliss, sheer unadulterated bliss. She would never have believed two people could achieve such closeness: never parted for more than an hour or two until now.

Travelling with him to wherever he needed to be, brief sojourns at the London apartment, attending glittering social events, longer periods here at the cottage, making it a real home, checking up on the youngsters up at the big house.

That had been her life up until now, and a wonderful life it was, too, she thought contentedly, lifting her face to the sun, breathing in the soft, clean, scented air. Tomorrow morning Ben would be home, and she would break the news, the news that she herself had found hard to believe.

For the first time ever she'd shaken her head when he'd invited her to hop on the company jet and fly with him to Amsterdam. A flash of disappointment had clouded his eyes at the thought of being parted for over a week. But then he'd grinned, 'What will you do with yourself?'

'Oh, this and that. Spend a few days shopping.' It was the first time she'd lied to him and it wasn't a good feeling. 'Then drive down to the cottage. Tackle the weeds before they swamp the garden.' That part at least was the gospel truth. 'Join me there?'

And so he would, tomorrow. She couldn't wait. Couldn't wait to tell him, to confess that she'd lied, to explain that it had been necessary because even she hadn't been able to absorb the truth.

Meanwhile, there was all that weeding to be done...

Two hours later Caroline got up off her knees, easing the stiffness out of her back. The sun was scorching her bare arms, and white cotton jeans hadn't been the ideal choice for a stint of dedicated gardening, she decided as she brushed ineffectually at the stains on her knees and tucked the straying hem of her ice-blue sleeveless shirt back beneath the waistband.

Hooking her hair behind her ears, she headed for shade; down the path, skirting the cottage and the meadow and through the gate in the picket fence. And she stood quite still in the clearing in the woods, then wandered down to the edge of the rushing stream.

She and Ben always spent time here when they were at the cottage. It was a sort of pilgrimage, she supposed, a ritual visit to their special place, the place they'd always come to on those long-ago soft summer nights.

They had so nearly lost each other. A shiver rippled her skin and then her breath caught in her throat. She hadn't heard him come but she knew he was here.

She spun round, her face alight, just as he entered the clearing.

'Ben!' She ran lightly towards him, into his arms, and he lifted her, spinning her round, then kissed her as if he was starving.

'I didn't expect you until tomorrow,' she uttered breathlessly when they both gulped in much needed air.

'I bunked off.' He grinned at her, ruffling her hair. 'You weren't inside, and you weren't in the garden—just all those weeds piled up on the paths which, no doubt, I shall be required to put on the compost heap. I knew you'd be here.'

Smiling, she kissed him again, and 'I've got something to tell you.'

They both spoke together. Caroline said, 'You first. Mine's got to be better than yours!'

'I wouldn't bet on that!' He drew her down onto the soft, mossy bank of the stream. 'Now, am I right in thinking you look on this place as our real home, our special place? I know I do.'

She nodded, mock serious, but her eyes were dancing. 'True. Is that it? Right, my turn!'

'Shh.' He laid a finger across her mouth to silence her. She nipped it with her teeth. Grinning, he told her, 'I wasn't too miffed when you said you didn't want to come to Amsterdam. I missed you like crazy but it did give me the opportunity to get things moving without you breathing down my neck. I wanted it done and dusted, then spring the surprise. I'm going to work mostly from home—here—in the future. No more jetting round the continent at the drop of a hat. Any travelling we do in the future will be for pleasure—holidays—in any part of the world that takes your fancy. Of course—' he traced the outline of her mouth with a delicate, sensual finger '—it will mean building on. Just a room to house the usual electronic communications systems. Is that OK with you?'

'Couldn't be better.' She looped her arms around his neck and gently touched his mouth with hers. 'It fits in so well with what I've got to tell you.'

'Which is?'

'I'm pregnant. I wasn't sure but now I am. I didn't go shopping, why should I? I have everything I could want or need. I had it confirmed. I had a scan.'

Ben just stared at her. Caroline said, 'Aren't you pleased?' knowing he had to be. She knew him as well as she knew herself. And he confirmed it, his face lighting up in the grin that had the power to stun her.

'I'm ecstatic, my precious darling! Over the moon! Well done, Caro!'

'It takes two,' she said, laughter lurking behind the prim expression she plastered on. 'And that's not all. We're expecting twins.'

A breathless, adoring hug later she emerged from encircling arms that would have held onto her for ever. 'We'll have to build on a rumpus room. And being country babies they'll grow up to want ponies. And that means building a stable, and fencing off a paddock. And if we have more we'll need another bedroom. Or two. And an extra bathroom. The place will just get bigger and bigger. Do you mind?'

For answer he slid an arm back round her waist and drew her down with him onto the soft mossy grass. 'I can put up with everything getting bigger—and better.' A softly stroking hand slid over her still flat tummy, commanding fingers finding the button of her waistband. 'Just like my love for you—bigger and better in every way, day by glorious day.'